1

Were:
A Secret World Novel

Kathryn Wyant

CHAPTER 1

The sunlight dappled leaves left over from last fall cushioned their footfalls. There was no wind to carry their scent to the herd of mule deer that were grazing on the sage below. Marcus called a halt to the pride's advance. "We can change here and have a very successful hunt."

An errant breeze whispered in the leaves above as they transformed. Four feet replaced two as short tawny fur covered them and gold eyes blinked in the sun as with a twist of his head and a shifting of his weight Marcus sat on his haunches. His thoughts were directed toward the dinner below. The pride spread out and moved down the hillside to nearly surround the herd of dinner on the hoof.

They rushed the herd of mule deer and the startled animals began to run. The yearling cats sped as quickly as they could and three of the females brought down a young buck that was too slow to take his elders' warning.

The male, Will, ran flat out after a wily large doe that zigzagged in her path and avoided being caught. He turned his sight to a lone male that seemed to be weaker than the others. He ran full tilt at the buck and leaped for his back. His claws sank deep onto his shoulders and he bit the back of the male's neck. As blood exploded in his mouth he felt the bones crunch beneath his powerful jaws and the buck collapsed beneath him.

Marcus watched closely as the young females and male made their first successful big game hunt. Yes, they would do well when they had finished growing. The four of them, three females and one male, had taken to their hunting lessons well. He sauntered down to the flat where the pride waited for him. He would begin to eat first and he chose a buck brought down by Rosa, his favorite female. Once he had begun to eat the rest of the pride joined in the feast. The three other older members of the pride who had made it to watch the hunt would feed well and once they transformed they would bring the rest of the kills to be butchered and frozen against the winter.

Their town boasted a great butcher shop where you could store your kills. It was run by a were bear, a heavy set six foot four inch tall Scotsman. There was a veterinarian, a grocery and several small shops including a dry goods store, two clothing stores and Marcus' book store. There were two pharmacies a second grocery store and three gas stations, a coffee shop, an ice cream parlor and four churches. The town had several time share complexes and a B and B as well as motels and the posh ski resort called Purgatory. The hotel there had a fine dining restaurant. There were also the usual bars and fast food places that catered to the tourist trade. During the ski season a French restaurant was open and so was a German style guest house. Finally, there was the Fox and Hound, an English style pub just outside of town

4

which had great beer, stout and ale. It was a
sanctuary where members of the were community
could relax and meet together regardless of their
affiliation. Were bears rubbed elbows with were
wolves and cats.

Marcus was very proud of his extended
family and their places in the town. Most of the
weres were either police officers, firemen or
emergency medical people and these last worked
for the local hospital. The were wolves were
mainly police officers, the bears were mainly
firefighters and the were cats were mainly medical
personnel. However there weren't that many of
them. Marcus' pride of twelve was the largest
group of were cats in the west. Rather than
keeping expanding he deliberately raised the
young to not hunt or bite humans unless they were
seen transforming. Of course they could say the
person was nuts but that didn't always suffice.
Especially if the person was well respected from
outside the community and there for the hunting,
skiing or hiking in the woods or to ride the narrow
gauge railroad in Durango.

Their town quadrupled in size during the
fall, winter and spring when skiing season was in.
It was then that the weres were at their most
vulnerable. They never knew who might be out
and about when the moon was full and the call to
change was dominating their bodies. They thought
about leaving and moving to cabins deep in the
north woods of British Columbia where they

would be free to change but they loved their creature comforts of hot showers and the like. They were the most hedonistic of the weres. They also had a range of five hundred square miles so they could drive to isolated areas for transforming.

They all lived together in a large old house that had once been a hotel when the Wells Fargo Stage came through on the way to California. They also had been a way station for the pony express riders who changed horses at the livery stable attached to the hotel.

The family was made up of Marcus two other adult males, two of his sisters, his wife a couple of cousins and everyone's children. The other male members, Charles and James, were wed to his sisters and so he tolerated them. He was fond of all of his pride members. There was a rumor that there was a lone cat living in a cabin just north of them but none of them had ever seen him. Then the body was found.

CHAPTER 2

The human had obviously been the victim of an attack by a large cat. The paw prints were obvious and led from the surrounding mountains. Marcus was one of the hunters requested by the sheriff. His tracking skills were unmatched by any except his brothers in law. He was busy putting together a display of the latest best sellers when the sheriff came in. "Good morning George. What can I do for you?"

"I'm afraid I'm going to have to ask you to bring your brothers in law over to the jail."

"How come George? What did they do this time? Speed again?"

"No we found a body and it was a cat kill. Marcus I know it was none of yours but I need to ask the boys and you to help track it."He looked hopefully at Marcus. "We are arranging a search party because it appears to have been injured at some point, one of the hind legs doesn't work quite right, Ski Patrol found the woman.

The body was that of a skier who had been going cross country and not on a marked trail. She had apparently wanted to be alone and to ski on pristine snow. When she didn't join her friends as arranged they had contacted the ski patrol and they found the body a few miles north of town.

It would be easier if the snow wasn't so messed up by the tracks from the deputies. They have muddied the scene and I cant find which ones are the original. And the damn cat tracks have disappeared."

"What do you mean disappeared?" That disturbed Marcus more than he was willing to show. "How can tracks just disappear?"

"Oh there are tracks coming and tracks there just none going. Of course this early in the season there isn't much snow under the pines. We figure the cat used that fact and disappeared."

7

"Oh I see what you mean. Well the boys and I will be happy to help. When do you want us to meet you and where."

"As soon as possible at the jail. We have a lot of volunteers coming from the next town and from here. I am surprised at the local volunteers. A lot of them are from out of town and are staying at the local motels and so forth."

"I'll call the house and have them meet us at the jail then. We should be there in half an hour."

CHAPTER 3

The cat watched from deep in the pines as the men in the orange jackets with backpacks found his kill. He licked more of the blood from his muzzle and with a smile of satisfaction leaped from snow free zone to snow free area. He knew he was going to get away with it. None of the townies could match him for nature wisdom that was sure.

He had moved down from British Columbia looking for a milder climate and easier hunting. The area of the San Juan Mountains was perfect. He had found an abandoned mine with a building that was secure enough to keep him out of the weather. He had cash from a previous kill and used it to buy blankets and cooking gear. The cash from his most recent kill would buy other necessities. The area had plenty of stupid humans.

He transformed and began to jog. He could keep up the pace for an hour or more and he knew he was in the clear. The stupid humans would never figure out who had killed the ignorant woman. It was then that he stepped wrong and felt his ankle twist at an unnatural angle. He fell and started swearing. The pain was immediate and searing. It was the same ankle he had broken and not had set properly several years ago. He crawled over to a fallen tree and pulled himself up to sit on it and check his ankle. Well at least nothing was broken but the sprain was going to slow him down considerably.

He took out his hunting knife and used it to cut a branch he could use as a crutch. Then he began to make his painful way to the old mine building. Climbing the stairs would be a bitch but he would be home free. He sat to rest and watch a wood pecker drill for insects. There was a hare crouched under a juniper and as he watched a coyote snuck up on him. The rabbit became aware if his danger too late. The cat in human form watched as the coyote broke its neck and then feasted.

Time to move before he stiffened up. He was becoming aware of further injuries. The pack with the meat he had taken from his victim was weighing heavy on his shoulders. He thought about changing but then how would he carry his meat home? No best to just tough it out so he struggled to his feet and plodded toward home. There were only a couple of miles to go when he became aware that there was something on his back trail. He had stopped for a breather beside a stream and had broken the ice to get a drink. He wasn't sure how he knew just something in his gut told him he needed to hurry and the meat be damned. He dropped the pack and transformed. He managed a three legged lope and made the cabin where he transformed and collapsed.

Marcus and his brother cats had spread out and his brother in law, James, picked up a partial boot track near the halfway point of their back trail. He whistled to the others and they joined him.

James transformed and began to cast back and forth. It wasn't long before he picked up the scent of human mixed with cat and they all realized they were indeed dealing with a renegade were of their species which meant it was up to them to kill it. This was their territory. They chose to share it with the wolves and the bears. They refused to share it with a non pride cat especially a renegade.

James located where the were had fallen and they traced his actions. The holes created by the improvised crutch made tracking simple so they ran. An hour later they discovered the backpack and the human meat at the stream. They followed the cat's trail to the cabin where they brought him to bay.

They shot him and then burned his body and the cabin to the ground. It was in bad shape having been abandoned for so long and within a short time was nothing but smoking rubble. His burned body would be found and it would be considered a tragic accident.

They transformed and ran back to near the other hunters where they returned to human form. They spoke to George then, telling him what they had found and about the "accidental fire". He agreed to say they had killed a mountain lion and buried the remains as the skin was too badly damaged to bring home. They couldn't have brought the skin anyway as he had been in human form when he died. Fortunately no one questioned their statements.

The hunting party returned to the town, cold and hungry so they went to the Fox and Hound for a hot toddy and some chili. The pub made the best chili in town and it was on their way home. They warmed up by the fire and then bravely reentered the cold for the final leg of their trip. Home was to the south of town nestled against a butte and surrounded by yellow pines and a few junipers they had planted for the berries. They got into the pickup and headed home.

The house was all one story and was made of adobe. It was very Spanish in design and everyone who saw it loved it. The cats were especially fond of their bedroom, which was one huge bed. There was room for everyone so they could cuddle and sleep or make love when the time was right or the spirit moved them.

It was getting dark when the truck pulled up in front of the wrap around porch. Warm yellow light spilled out of the windows welcoming them home. They could smell dinner cooking and welcomed the aroma of roasted chicken.

One of the wives raised the chickens and another raised sheep and goats. They didn't try to raise cattle or horses because their smell was frightening to the creatures. One of the wives opened the door and rubbed against them in welcome as they came in. The eldest, Marcus' wife asked about the hunt and the others gathered close to hear his answer. He went into great detail so they could feel a part of the experience. When they got to the part about killing the renegade and burning the cabin the family were suitably impressed by the hunters' solution to the problem of disposal. And then it was time for dinner.

They ate in silence each one occupied with filling empty bellies. When dinner was over the younger cats cleared the table and washed the dishes. They also checked the pantry to see if there were enough canned goods to last or whether they would have to go to town to one of the grocery stores. Their garden was small but generally yielded enough vegetables, and that included asparagus, to feed the pride over the winter.

Shopping would not be necessary. Spring would be there soon enough. With it the tourists would leave temporarily.

CHAPTER 4

Spring arrived and with the warmer weather came the births of the newest generation of weres. Marcus' family was the exception. Their youngest had been born in the fall and she already was a handful. She crawled everywhere and she was quick. If her babysitter looked away for a moment she would scoot to under the dining table and hide while her watcher pretended to look everywhere for her. She would giggle then and of course the sitter would act surprised to see her. It was one of her favorite games, that and being in the kitchen while the family made things with delicious smells. She occasionally got to have a fresh cookie which she loved. She had enough teeth to chew her food and she loved getting treats from whoever was baking.

Her name was Christine and she was doted on by her father, Charles or maybe Marcus. She had the same goldish brown eyes as her mother and the same tawny gold hair as her father. Her features were even and very lovely and her older cousins called her their princess and spoiled her every chance they had. It was unfortunate to her mind as spoiling was seldom due to their daily chores before and after school. So they were relegated to spoiling her on weekends. Marcus doted on her more than anyone else although her primary care was by her mother Alice. She rarely saw Charles and decided he couldn't be her dad.

As she grew she took full advantage of her position as every ones' favorite and she enjoyed getting her cousins to wait on her. By age four she had figured out how to get her way with non pride members too. She always behaved with the utmost decorum when adults were present. However when they were absent she ruled the other young with quick claws. Marcus was aware of her tendencies and was grooming her to be the pride's lead female. There was one male cousin, William, she couldn't control because he was older and bigger and he was being groomed to take over for Marcus.

CHAPTER 5

They were in their late teens and had graduated from the local high school. Both had graduated with three point nine grade point averages and had been accepted at the nearby college on the bluff above Durango. They lived in an apartment complex within easy walking distance of the campus and usually spent their mornings trying to beat the other to class, William, called Will, generally won which Christine blamed on needing to fix her hair and put on her makeup.

William just told her to get up earlier. He would tease her to the point where she was too angry to respond and then he would do something charming like buying her flowers or chocolate covered cherries so she always forgave him.

They were actually very close and in some ways Christine, Chris to her friends, adored him. He was honorable and always told the truth. He had a fine set of ethics and would help anyone who needed it and yet he was still a bit aloof from most people. Chris figured it was because he was were like her.

Chris was finally in bed for the night, by the time she had finished her shift at the bar it was two am and she was glad her first class wasn't until one. For some reason William was on her mind. She thought about when they both changed for the first time and how scared she had been. Oh she had been told what to expect and she had seen her relatives change but that wasn't the same as experiencing it herself.

She had gone into woods surrounding their house when her change began. Fortunately her cousin Will had known something was happening to her and her found her. He talked her through the discomfort and the horrible itching. She could see why some weres didn't make it. The stress was enormous on the heart. She remembered how when she had changed back Will had held her and soothed her jagged nerves. He really was a dear and she wished he felt for her what she felt for

15

him. At twelve she was sure they would make a
perfect couple. Well maybe someday. Of course
that had been years ago and she had nearly given
up on that dream.

She fell asleep and dreamed of Will. In her
dream they were lying in a meadow high in the
mountains near their home when Will picked a
lupine and drew it down her nose and over her lips.
The flower trailed down her throat and between
her breasts and over her bare stomach. Her reached
for the buttons on her blouse and slowly began to
undo them. He paused between each one to see if
she would stop him. When she sighed and didn't
he continued. He gently separated the halves of the
belly shirt and exposed her breasts to the sky. The
cool breeze made her nipples crinkle and she
reached up to play with the hair on the back of his
neck. He leaned over and slowly approached her
mouth. When he kissed her she felt a tingle in her
passion bud. She reached up and undid the buttons
on his shirt. Her fingers played with the hair she
found there and she saw his nipples bud. She
licked one and he groaned and kissed her again
then his mouth moved down over her jaw to her
throat and he teased the flesh with his tongue. She
responded with a moan. His lips and tongue trailed
further down and found her breasts. As he nuzzled
them he licked the tips of her nipples causing her
to squirm with desire. His hand trailed down and
found the buttons of her jeans. He slipped each one
from its seat and gently pulled them down. She

16

raised her hips to allow him to draw them off and he sat up on his heels to remove them completely. He had left her lace high rise panties in place. He trailed his hand up her calf and thigh to touch the moist fabric. She was ready for him. As she twisted with her need he quickly unfastened his jeans and stood to kick them off. His shaft was hard and ready to spear her to her core. She smiled at him and whispered "please." He pulled her panties off quickly. He lay down between her waiting thighs and his shaft nudged her passion bud as he slid home. They began the dance that led to the stars then and as his tempo sped up her moans of desire became a shout of "Yes!" as she exploded and sailed to the heavens above. He was right there with her and as they drifted in completion they kissed and nibbled each others lips and throats. "Thank you beautiful." Will said. "You are wonderful and I adore you."

Chris went deeper into sleep and was unaware of the shadow that jumped from her second floor balcony and disappeared into the night.

Will had been aware that something was happening to Chris that involved making love but he thought it was real and was ready to kill the male who was trespassing on what he considered his. When he realized she was dreaming he was shocked at the intensity of the jealousy he felt for her dream lover. When she settled into deeper sleep he jumped from her balcony and went home

17

to his apartment in the next building. He felt
shaken by what he had experienced. It was time to
tell Chris how he felt. But how to do it without
sounding lame! He would have to plan things very
carefully.
Lame was easy, cool was not and more than
anything he wanted to seem cool to Chris.

CHAPTER 6

Chris woke languidly and stretched. She
got up and padded naked into her bathroom for her
morning shower. She was amazed at how relaxed
she felt and grinned thinking about her glorious
night. She wished, not for the first time, that those
glorious nights with Will were real. She wondered
how to let him know how she felt without
sounding lame. She would have to be very careful
and not let him see what he did to her emotionally
and how he turned her on by just smiling at her.
One way she could do it would be to pretend to be
a little drunk, but then he wouldn't believe her. He
was also too honorable to take advantage of her. It
would definitely take a lot of thought and
planning. She sighed.
Shower finished she dried off and got
dressed in jeans and a sweater that hugged her
curves. She made coffee then and had her rye toast
with it. She collected the books and notebooks she
would need for her two afternoon classes and left

her apartment. She climbed the hill covered with junipers and walked past the married student housing. On her right was the football field with its broadcast booth and bleachers. Next came one of the science buildings and beside that was her class for Intro to Geology. She didn't see Will and figured he was already inside.

She found him in his usual seat in the front row and sat next to him. "Good morning."

"Don't you mean afternoon?"

Chris laughed, "Yes I suppose I could. But since I only woke up an hour ago it is still morning to me."

"How come you slept so long? Did you have a bad night?"

"No actually I had a great night." She grinned a gamine smile. "Yes a very great night indeed."

Will started to question her but their professor called the class to order and began taking roll call. The lecture was on Igneous rocks and vulcanism. He said they should read the chapter on plate tectonics and that there would be a test on Monday on everything in today's lecture and the chapters in their texts that dealt with the same. "Class dismissed."

Psychology was next and Chris found it fascinating. When class was dismissed Will asked her, "You want to go for lunch then? Or breakfast? I'll buy."

"Since you asked and you're buying, sure. I'm hungry."

"You want to go to the union or down town to the coffee shop?"

"Let's go to the coffee shop."

"Come on then we'll take my car."

"When did you get a car?"

"Yesterday. It's a MG Spider in blue."

"Oh how fun!"

They found the car and Chris hopped in while Will fished out his keys and told her to put on her seat belt. It was an old enough car that it didn't need a chest belt. The blue was a rich royal blue and Chris loved it. She looked at Will, her eyes shining, "Thank you Will." She was aware that her heart was there in her eyes for him to see. But he didn't look and so the moment passed.

The coffee shop was surprisingly empty when they arrived and they decided it was because it was mid-afternoon. They picked a seat by the windows where they could see the river and watch the ducks diving for food. They watched silently while they waited for the server to bring them menus and take their order for coffee.

"I'm sorry I didn't see you come in. What can I get you?"

"Menus and coffee to start," Will said.

"Coming right up." She grabbed a couple of menus and a coffee pot and brought both to the table. Within seconds they had coffee. The menus provided lunch specials as well as the regular menu selections. "I'll be back in a few minutes so you have time to decide on what you want to eat." She hustled away to roll clean silverware into napkins. She situated herself so she could watch Chris and Will so she could refill their cups and know when they had decided on what to eat. Soon enough they put their menus down and she hustled to their table.

Orders for eggs and toast given Chris and Will settled in for a review of the psychology lecture they had just heard and how it compared to the chapter they had read in the text.

"I agree that Freud put too much emphasis on female hysteria and sexuality, We are much more than the urge to reproduce or have sex with our fathers."

"We are not all attracted to our opposite sex parent either."Will stated flatly.

"The prof didn't say that, though he seemed to support Freud and his idea that humans are essentially sexual beings."

"Whatever, I think Freud was a bit off track to say the least."

They argued the merits and detriments of Freudian psychology while they ate and then Chris said, "Well what about the Jung's Archetypes. I am surprised Freud didn't develop a theory about them considering the emphasis he had on Electra and Oedipus."

"Good point. But Jungian Archetypes are not sexuality based. They are personality types."

21

"Oh I haven't read the chapter on Jung yet. But I have read Rogers."

"I like a lot of what he has to say." Their conversation was mostly about Psychological theories and then Chris said, "But their location geographically has a bearing too, you know and so does the language they speak."

"How do you mean?"

"Well some concepts are slightly different and the mental picture a word gives influences how a person hears it. For example the word wind brings to mind a particular type of breeze. Some may see a hurricane wind while others see a gentle summer zephyr, see what I mean? Any people up north will see a cold wind while those in the south will see a warm one. Or the word tree or water or...well you get the picture. Emotional words will be the same based on life experiences. Those experiences will color how they act and react to stimulus."

"Language as a psychological tool?"

"Yeah, sort of. I think it helps with diagnosis or at least with developmental psychology."

"Cool."

They talked about their Asian History class notes next and then it was time to pay the bill and leave. Will was interested in exploring Chris' developmental psychology idea and thought she should write a paper based on it. Who knew, she might even publish a book about it.

They rode back to the dorms and Will asked, "So what are you doing Friday night? Got a date?"

"No, why?"

"I thought maybe you would like to go to dinner and a movie with me."

"Really? You mean like a date?"

"Yeah, if you want to?"

Chris was shocked since Will usually had a date with his steady. "What about Cindy?"

"We're not seeing each other any more. She said I was boring."

"She's stupid. Yeah I would really like to go out with you. I guess we have a lot in common and so I'm boring too." Without thinking Chris hugged Will and got a surprising tingle. All she could think of was that it was a good thing they were only second cousins and not closer relations, so she could seduce him. They soon became a steady couple but Chris regretfully remained a virgin even though eight days every month she felt the need for sexual fulfillment more strongly than the rest of the time. Will maintained his distance.

CHAPTER 7

They became inseparable and moved in together soon after graduation, Chris had a degree in psychology and Will had one in geology. Will went to work for the USGS, United States

Geologic Survey based out of Denver so they weren't too far from their pride lands.

Every year Will spent most of his time in The San Juan Mountains mapping the strata of sedimentary and metamorphic rocks found there. Chris would join him for weekends and her vacation. Then they would take Will's data back to Denver to draw up detailed maps of the areas he had walked across during the other six months of the year.

While they were in the San Juans and Uncompahdres they spent some of their nights back home. And it was during one of their nights there that they decided to go back to school for their masters and doctorates. They had already saved enough money to do it. They were both grade six government employees but they wanted to be more and that took education and dedication.

One day in early Spring, they got the letters saying they had been accepted at Fort Lewis College in Durango for the Geology post graduate program and the doctoral program in psychology. They celebrated by going for a run in the forests of Pike's Peak outside Denver. They had a house in Lakewood which was close to the USGS headquarters there. They had been fortunate in buying the house as it was situated on a full acre of land with a back yard that was big enough to build another house on. Their next-door neighbors to the south had a horse and the neighbors to the north had a huge garden. They decided to cultivate their

24

back yard in sections. They divided it into yard then flower beds then vegetable garden then more yard where they played badminton and croquet. They had a stone patio nestled in the angle of the Ell outside the back door that extended halfway down the long arm of the Ell of the house under the bedroom windows. They planted a forsythia at the edge of the patio that ended where the master bedroom windows stopped. Around the shrub they planted some ferns and crocuses there were intermittent daffodils too which echoed the yellow of the forsythia. In the room next their bedroom they set up an office with a drafting table for adding details to the maps Will used at work.

For their garden they planted vegetables that they could can for the winter just like at home, and they planted flowers that appealed to Chris like varieties of iris. They also planted garlic and chives. They had a garden window in the kitchen where they planted herbs in pots.

Once they moved to Durango they moved into married student housing on the campus. They brought their indoor garden with them. Since they shared a last name there were no questions. Their love just kept growing and they finally consummated it on their first night in the new apartment. Chris began it by dancing for Will. It was a slow seductive dance to Ravel's Bolero and by the time she was done they were both breathing hard. Will's shaft was so hard it was difficult to stand and her nipples were crinkled nubs. She reached out and stroked his face and he rubbed against her palm rather like a big house cat.

Chris moved then to stand between his spread knees and he reached up to caress her hips and sides his hands gradually moving forward and up to caress her breasts.

She sighed with pleasure her hands going to play with the hair on the back of his neck. She leaned down then and drew his face up so she could kiss him, one hand staying to play with his hair the other sliding down to caress his chest. When he deepened the kiss she slid her hand down to touch the prominent bulge in his jeans. He moaned into her mouth and let his tongue play with hers. He pulled away far enough to ask her if she was sure and at her convulsive nod he began to unbutton the shirt she was wearing. The air was warm against her and she gloried in the slightly rough skin of his hands in contrast to the satin feel of the air.

He slid the shirt down her arms and let it drop onto the rug. Then he kissed the inside of her elbow and ran his tongue down to her palm where he traced the lines. The touch sent shivers of pleasure through her to tingle in her passion's bud. Then he licked her stomach and his hands unfastened her lacy bra. He licked her breasts in spirals ending at the nipples where he suckled gently.

Chris nearly exploded from the sensual contact. She moaned and pinched his nipples. His shaft jerked against the restraint of his jeans and he moved to unbutton and unzip them. His erection was painful in its intensity and he sighed as Chris touched it. His hands were busy with the buttons on her jeans and she could barely wait to feel his rod inside her. She shoved his jeans down his muscular thighs and the bent to kiss the tip of his shaft. Her jeans were soon in a pile around her ankles and she pulled her feet out and kicked them aside. Her eagerness to make love was only equaled by his and as moisture dewed the tip of his love rod she licked it to enjoy the salty sweet taste. He groaned then and begged her to give him release. She laughed then and jumped to wrap her legs around his hips pushing him off balance to fall onto the bed.

His shaft was pinned against her cleft and she moved back and forth on it increasing her need and his. He grasped her waist and raised her so that she hung suspended above the rampant rod and he slowly lowered her onto it until he felt resistance.

"You are a virgin?" He whispered.

"Not after tonight." She whispered back and she kissed his neck and licked upward to kiss his jaw and then his lips. Her tongue darted out to lick them. Will deepened their kiss and as he did so he thrust once hard breaking through the delicate barrier. The pain was momentary and intense enough to cause her to shout into his mouth. He held her still for a few moments to allow her time to recover and then he began to

27

thrust slowly nearly leaving her sheath then gently
and slowly sending the sword home. She moaned
with her need and began to speed up her motion.
He met her thrust for thrust and soon they were
transported to the heavens above. The culmination
of their passion was like fireworks and transported
them to the stars where they could not tell where
each began or ended. The moments of rapture
lasted for it felt like forever and Chris cried with
happiness. "I never knew it could be like this. Oh I
love you so much I can't express it in words."

"You are my beloved and I will never let
you go." Will murmured. They lay at peace so
profound that it was with regret that Chris got up
to get a wet towel and a dry one so she could
cleanse Will. She sang as she went and came back.
"Thank you my love. That was incredible."

"You are amazing."

"Thank you. I think that if it is always like
that it is no wonder the bed at home is always so
busy."

"It isn't."

Chris climbed back into bed and snuggled
against Will. "You mean it isn't always this
good?"

"What we shared was phenomenal."

"Oh, I'm glad." She yawned silently.

"Me too." Will kissed her, "Thank you
Beauty."

"You're welcome, Beast."

"I think we will be doing this more often now that we know how great it is. What do you think?"

Her answer was a soft purry snore. He lay awake for a short time and blessed whatever gods might be listening that they had finally found each other. Then he too slept. His dreams echoed hers and were filled with the playful games that lovers play.

CHAPTER 8

Their classes were difficult and it took a lot of Will's attention to memorize the names of different strata of rocks. He learned about the fault lines that crisscrossed the mountains and foot hills. They relearned which symbols to use when mapping and drawing up charts. These were the same ones they had used in Will's work at the USGS and Chris had helped him.

Then it was winter and they spent Christmas at home with Marcus and the rest of the pride. Marcus arranged a Solstice Hunt for them. It was wonderful. They brought down an elk which they thought didn't belong that far south.

The haunches would make for excellent roasts for their solstice dinner. And the vegetables they had frozen that fall would make an excellent addition to the meal. For afters they had orange cake with home made orange icing.

After dinner they sat around the fireplace and told Marcus about school and that they would like to be married. Marcus and the others were delighted and the women immediately began planning a Spring wedding. Charles and Alice were particularly pleased as was James, Will's father.

They elected to have their marriage occur in June after they graduated and the pride was expected to come. Will and Chris were the first members of the pride to go to college and to achieve doctorates. Marcus hoped they would serve as a model for the teen-aged members of the extended family.

June came and Chris invited the members of the were community as well as their friends from college. Even two strangers came uninvited to attend their marriage. The service was being held in the grove of aspens that was on the pride's farm. There was no need for decorative flowers from the flower shop as the iris were in bloom and so were the columbine and other wild flowers. The colors Chris had chosen were pale green and white. The green of her gown made her look like a wood nymph. As she walked toward Will he thought no one could be more beautiful and graceful. They met beneath the aspen surrounded by their guests and family and told each other their vows then the local judge pronounced them wed according to the laws of Colorado and introduced them to everyone as Mr. and Mrs. William Richard Deleon.

The reception was at the local grange hall where the pride's females had gone earlier to decorate.

There were garlands of wild flowers gracing the spaces between the windows and there were crepe paper garlands from the center light to the walls of the hall. The raised stage was one step higher than the main part of the floor and it was there that James and his wife, Marcus and his wife, Rosa and Will and Chris sat with Charles and Alice at a long table all facing the dance floor. Their table had a white table cloth and was decorated with wild flowers and ivy. The crystal, and silverware gleamed in the candle light as they took their seats. Around the perimeter of the room other tables and chairs were set for the rest of the wedding guests. Marcus put in a CD and music wafted over them in a soft background to the quiet talk.

It was time for the toasts and Will's best friend from school gave the first humorous speech. He mentioned how flustered Will had been that morning and how hung over he was from the bachelor party of the night before. He talked about the girl who came out of the cake and danced for them as she stripped and how Will didn't know how to deal with it. He also mentioned Will's lack of success with the girls at school which was a blatant falsehood. Chris laughed and then it was the maid of honor's turn. She made everyone laugh when she told them about Chris' embarrassment with the male stripper they had brought in from Denver. And how she had no clue about how to handle him. Everyone including Will and Chris laughed at the story and about how she had told her professor that Freud was an idiot. There were lots of amusing anecdotes.

Will kissed her and everyone applauded. Then it was time for food. The were women had all made their most popular dishes for the potluck buffet. Will and Chris led the way along it to serve themselves from the bounty there. They had three different vegetables and salads including a fruit salad, and chili and barbecued ribs and roast elk along with potatoes done four different ways, three hot and one cold. There were burgers and hotdogs and all sorts of casseroles and fun foods and then it was time to cut the cake.

Chris had ordered it from the baker and it was indeed spectacular. It was four tiers separated with columns and topped with modeling chocolate wild flowers. There was a champagne fountain. A chocolate one which they found at the local rental place was served with the strawberries they had found at their favorite local grocery store. It was an excellent feast. The party grew noisy as people drank the wine and mixed drinks from the open bar. But surprisingly there were no fights, or if there were they were outside.

By midnight everyone was either too drunk to drive or they were gone. Will and Chris had slipped away a little earlier. They went to the local airport where a single engine plane flew them to the Stapleton International Airport in Denver. They caught a plane to Miami Executive Airport and from there flew first class to the Bahamas for their honeymoon.

CHAPTER 9

They landed and were first off the plane. The warmth of the air was a shock after the chill of the air-conditioned plane. The sun was just rising and the sky was a beautiful pale blue and the clouds were gold and peach with a hint of lavender. The air under the smell of the Jet fuel was redolent with the perfume of the flowers and beneath that was a hint of rotting vegetation. There were smells of cooking also in the air and Will and Chris sniffed appreciatively. Eyes sparkling with excitement they took a rental car and drove to their hotel, Atlantis Paradise Resort. They entered from the dim early morning into a warm golden glow. Chris was amazed at the twenty plus foot ceiling and the intricate art of the highly polished floor. There were huge carved columns that looked like alabaster and above were colorful murals of scenes straight out of mythology. The circular room had the registration desk where Will signed the cards for both of them and then they were escorted to their room on the top floor of the hotel.

Their room's sliding glass doors and balcony looked out over the beautiful azure water of the sea and the white sand beach below. The room held a huge king sized bed large enough to play on and a sitting area with a couch, chairs, television, and tables including a dining table and chairs. There was a champagne bottle chilling in a bucket of ice and there were strawberries to feed each other. The colors were warm golds, oranges and yellows with abstract patterned decorative pillows for the bed and couch.

After tipping their bellman, Will closed the drapes making the room dark and then he approached Chris a rumble in his throat. The need to change and have sex was affecting him strongly as a result of Chris being in heat so she changed to cat form. She rubbed against his legs and felt him begin to change so she bounded onto the bed and presented to him. He finished changing and was on her in a flash. They made love for the first time in their were forms and Chris decided that although it was good, human form was better because there was more variety in position possible. Although it was tempting to cuddle in cat form and to sleep that way they changed back to human. It would not do for a maid to come into the room while they were cats.

Will went to the bathroom and got the accouterments to clean himself and Chris. Then they cuddled and fell asleep. They slept until it was daylight again and decided that it would be fun to go through the underwater tunnel and view the local fish. But that was for after breakfast. First they would shower together and make love in the water. The shower heads were the type that made bathing like being in the rain.

Breakfast was room service. Mimosas began it then Eggs Benedict and assorted tropical fruit. Mangoes and guava predominated. The coffee was marvelous and tasted like pure Colombian heaven. "Lets go on a tour of the complex today."

"That sounds like a great idea, but I for sure want to check out the under sea tunnel. I love the look of tropical fish."

"I agree, they are so colorful and there are so many different kinds."

"Oh I hear you. And I want to try the water slides, they look like great fun."

"What about parasailing? And board surfing? Oh and paddle boarding?"

"Ooh that sounds like fun too."

"Well we have a week to do everything so I suggest we take our time and maybe do one thing a day. The rest of the time we can lay in the sun and come up here to make love."

"I like the way you think." They looked fondly at each other.

They did everything that was available to try while they were there. Strangely enough they ran into the two strangers from their wedding who claimed to be vacationing. It seemed odd to Will but he didn't share his concerns with Christine.

It seemed all to soon their week was up and it was time to fly back to Colorado. They looked tanned and fit and with their blond streaked hair and golden brown eyes they made a memorable couple. They had also been very generous in tipping the staff that took care of their needs. The resort employees were a little sad to see them go.

Their flight chased the sun back to Colorado and Stapleton Airport. They lost the race and the plane landed in the dusk. The shadows of the mountains had covered the city but the sky was still light and the sunset colors of the clouds were almost as spectacular as those they had seen from Atlantis. But was more satisfying because they were driving home. When they arrived they had missed dinner so they went to the Fox and Hound where they were greeted with hugs.

Charles, James and Marcus were there having a companionable drink and had not expected them for another day. "You look like your trip was beneficial."

"Yes indeed, and we are happy for you. Where did you go?"

"We went to Atlantis in the Bahamas and it was amazing. We had a wonderful time. Did anything exciting happen while we were gone?"

"Oddly enough nothing of note."

"Well that's good to hear, I would hate to have missed out on any excitement."Will said. Then they grabbed a table and had bistro style sandwiches for their dinner, meanwhile Marcus said,"No worries there. We'll see you at home."

CHAPTER 10

"Now tell us all about your trip." By this time they were home and ensconced around the fire pit where the youngest and oldest were toasting marshmallows.

"We tried all sorts of activities, like parasailing and that was scary and fun at the same time. You suddenly are airborne and you feel like you are flying..."

"Well you are."

"And everything gets small below you and you can see a slight curve to the horizon if you get high enough. I didn't get that high.

"I did. It was amazing." This from Will.

"The sky is so blue and the water is multicolored. An azure close to the shore and then deeper blue as you move put to deeper sea. It turns so dark it is like a deep midnight blue."

"True but closer in the water is so clear you can see the fishes and coral and there are sharks and I saw a manta ray too."

We also went to the undersea aquarium where you walk in a tunnel under the sea and see the fish up close and personal. And there are great carvings and the main lobby has these amazing murals. We took tons of pictures and as soon as they come back to CVS we will show you."

"Yeah cause words aren't enough."

"Did we mention the strangers from the wedding were there?"

"No, they were?"

"Yeah, they were on vacation supposedly."

"Supposedly?"

"Yes, although it seemed odd to me that they came to the wedding and then showed up at our honeymoon."

"Well I think it could have been coincidence."James said.

"You still believe in coincidence?"Marcus frowned at James.

"Sure don't you?"

"No. I don't, especially when it concerns my family."

Charles agreed with Marcus. A few days after that conversation they saw the strangers again. And this time they came right up to Charles and Will and said, "We are Michael and Richard Deleon and we represent an organization that you will find interesting. Would you introduce us to Marcus?"

"Where are you staying?"

"Purgatory Ski Resort North of Hesperus. Why?"

"We will have Marcus contact you there then."

Michael and Richard looked at each other and nodded. "It is good to see you are as cautious as we thought you were. We have been watching you since nineteen sixty four. And we finally decided it was time to meet. We represent a group you may have heard of. The ISPS. It's the International Society for the Preservation of the Supernatural or the Protection depending on your point of view."

"I haven't heard of you but Marcus may have."

"As the leader of your pride I would expect so, we have been around for a very long time. We work to protect the secret world."

"Why do you want to talk to my Uncle?"

"That is for your uncle to tell you, if he chooses, youngster."

Will started to bristle and then he realized that as his elder the man deserved respect so instead of saying anything stupid he said, "Yes sir."

At which, Michael smiled at him and said, "Good decision."surprising Will. "We will wait to hear from Marcus then."

Will and Charles finished their shopping and drove back to the ranch house. Will couldn't wait to tell Marcus about their encounter and to ask what the ISPS was about and why the rest of the pride didn't know of them. But he would have

39

to wait as Marcus was not in the compound. He decided to discuss the encounter with Chris only to find she was off with Marcus. "Well damn!" He complained to no one. "Why did they pick now to be gone!" He huffed a bit and decided a run would calm him down, so he changed into sweats and his running shoes and grabbed a bottle of water from the fridge in the kitchen, kissed his Aunt Rosa and jogged out the back door. He ran for a while and when he felt calm he turned to go home. The sun was setting behind the Uncompahdres when he walked into the yard and saw a couple of townee cars as well as the sheriff's jeep in front of the house. He hurried his steps then. His news could wait.

CHAPTER 11

Will entered a confusing bustle in the kitchen. He caught his aunt Rosa by the arm as she hurried past. "What's going on?"

"Ask your uncle or your father," She pulled away, "I'm too busy getting together a dinner for extra people at the last minute to talk."

Will was bumped from behind by one of his other aunts, "Hey kiddo, move it or lose it!" Will decided that leaving would be prudent.

As he went through the swinging door between the dining room and the kitchen he saw the three female cousins busily setting the table with the good silverware and china.

He walked into the den in time to hear, "So we wondered if they had contacted you too."

"No, not as of now but I expect to hear from them soon."

"Well Marcus the ISPS is very secret and they are very particular about who they contact."

"Which is why they contacted me in my bar last night when we were so busy." Henry, leader of the Bear Clan said with heavy irony.

"Be that as it may their members are generally not known outside the membership."

"Unless you screw up."

"Well there is that!" The sheriff said.

"Now about the water situation..."

Will decided it was time to interrupt, "Excuse me I am sorry to interrupt but we have been contacted by ISPS and they are waiting at Purgatory Ski Resort to hear from you Marcus. Their names are Michael and Richard Deleon so I think they must be distant cousins of ours."

"They are European?" At Will's nod Marcus said "Um. Possibly from Iberia or the other mountains like the Urals. They will be lynx or possibly lions who have migrated from Africa or Asia. Goodness knows there are enough people who emigrated from there to here or to Africa."

"What do you think they want with us?"

"Well I suspect much but I will wait until I speak with them before I start speculating out loud." Marcus laughed then and said, "Now what about the water? We have the Animus River after all."

Will left them to their deliberations and went in search of Chris to tell her about meeting Michael and Richard in town.

He found Chris in the living room watching TV and joined her to cuddle on the couch after a heartfelt kiss. She was watching the news and then switched over to one of the home renovation shows she loved...Good Bones. He told her about his encounter and the interaction between Marcus and him and about the new relations.

"Sweetheart? Maybe you should shower and change from your sweats for dinner?"

"Um, good idea. Want to join me?"

"And then we would miss dinner! No way my dear I'm hungry. You go clean up and I will wait for you back here."

"I'll be quick." Will was as good as his word and within half an hour he was back beside Chris on the couch. She was still watching Good Bones. She loved the designs they came up with and the interplay between the mother and daughter. It was very like the interactions she had with Marcus and Rosa and Charles and Maggie.

She was dressed for dinner in a dress which, due to the company, was dressier than her usual sweater and slacks. Will joined her in more formal attire too than his usual jeans and t-shirt. He was wearing a shirt with a collar and a tie with his jeans. "You look beautiful Chris." he smiled appreciatively. "Maybe we should have dinner guests more often."

Chris laughed, "You look rather handsome yourself, but, no, not a good idea. I would rather have dressing up be a surprise."

"Good point."

Chris laughed, "Well of course it is! I thought of it!"

"Very funny."

"Naturally. But now it is time to eat and I'm starving. It is what happens when you eat for two."

"What?"

"What do you mean what! I'm eating for two."

"We're pregnant?"

"That is generally the idea when one is eating for two, silly man."

"That is the best...the most exciting...I am so happy!" Will picked her up and swung her in a circle. "You are the most remarkable woman!"

"Yes, but now I need to eat before I perish from hunger."

"Who else knows?"

"No one. You alone. I thought you should hear first daddyo. I figure you can tell Marcus and Rosa and whoever else you think needs to know later. Can we please go in to dinner?" This last was said plaintively.

"Gods yes. And I will tell Marcus that he is going to be a grandfather after dinner and our guests leave."

"Who all is here?"

"The sheriff George, and Henry from the Fox and Hound and a representative from the Fey."

"The fey? They are usually so standoffish! I wonder what is up?"

"I don't know but I expect we will find out after dinner and they leave."

The dinner gong sounded then and they left the living room to join the others to go in to dinner and general conversation. Even the fey unbent a bit and chatted about inconsequentialities and doings in the forest. Their guests left after a postprandial brandy and Marcus said, "OK you two what has you bursting to tell me?"

"Well grandpa you might want to sit down while we tell you."

Marcus sat and then it dawned on him what they had called him."Grandpa? Really? Who else knows my dear girl?"

"Just us. I will be setting up an appointment to see Cousin Miranda since she is our OB Gyn specialist."

"You know that you will have to fight the change while you are expecting otherwise you will miscarry."Marcus hastened to tell her, "Changing puts too much strain on the body and with the strain of pregnancy it is just too much to tolerate."

"No I didn't know! I was going to suggest a hunt to celebrate." Will said, "Thank god you told us before hand."

"I would have wanted to change soon for a hunt anyway. Thank you Marcus."

"You will find it harder and harder not to change as your pregnancy progresses. We are not sure why but our medical people seem to think it is hormonal."

"It is a good thing I have strong wont power then."

"Wont power?"

"Sure I wont do something as opposed to I will do something. Wont power or will power."

"Wont power...I like that."

They lapsed into silence then until Marcus said "Will you tell Rosa or do you want me to do it?"

"Oh I want to so I can see her face."

"Understood. I would like to be there for the same reason."

"I thought to tell her with breakfast. Around seven or so. How will that work for you."

"Um, I can have a late breakfast. No problem there."

"Good, well good night then I'll see you in the morning." Chris kissed his cheek and left for bed and some serious cuddling. Fortunately she didn't show any outward sign that she was expecting so no one would comment on a baby bump. That would come later when she actually started to show. She snuggled into the curve of Wills belly and fell asleep.

Chris woke to feel Will's morning erection nudging her from the rear and she wriggled against him. "Woman you are dangerous." Will whispered in an effort not to wake any of the others. Chris turned on her back and threw the leg closest to Will over his hips. She guided his hard cock into her moist center and began to move from side to side.

"That's why you love me, "She whispered back. There was movement from others in the pile of bodies as others woke to their morning needs, some for sex and some for the bathroom.

Will and Chris orgasmed together and lay in the afterglow. She sighed with contentment then and kissed Will. "I love you Will."

"I love you too Chris. Are you ready to shower and then have breakfast?"

"I don't know, what time is it?"

"Nearly seven why?"

"We'll have to shower after breakfast then because Marcus wanted to be present with us this morning when we tell Rosa our news. He is waiting breakfast for us to join him."

"Oh well lets get dressed and we can go. We were supposed to be there when?"

"Around seven."

"Best hurry then." And they got up and dressed in record time. They made it to the dining room only ten minutes late. Marcus was just filling his first cup of coffee when they came running in. "Good morning Marcus." Will said as Chris kissed his cheek.

"Good morning you two. How did you sleep?"

Chris giggled, "Very well. You?"

"Also well. Rosa will be in in a few minutes to see what we want for breakfast. Will you tell her then before the others come in?"

"Yes, I had thought to. Although I don't mind the others knowing. They'll find out soon enough when I start to show."

"Beware one of the aunts and two of the cousins as they will be very jealous. The aunt has miscarried several times and so have the cousins. They couldn't resist the urge to change, you know what that means."

"Yes you made it very clear. Good morning Rosa."

"Good morning dear, what does everyone want for breakfast?"

"I'm not sure grandmother, what are you having grandfather?"

"Grandmother? I'm your mother... your mother...grandmother indeed! Grandmother?" Her eyes suddenly went wide as she realized what she was being called. A huge smile creased her cheeks, flushed red from the heat of the bread oven. She bustled around the table to lift Chris into a hug, "How far along are you? I'll have to plan a shower and go shopping with you and I am sure the midwife will need to be told and your personal doctor and the aunts and cousins will need to know too and...Oh there is so much to do. How far along did you say you were?"

Chris laughed. "Only eight weeks so there is plenty of time to do everything. I suggest we let the others find out on their own unless you think it would be better to tell them now before it becomes obvious."

"Tell them now so they have time to get used to it and over any resentment and jealousy before your baby comes."

Chris heard a gasp and her aunt Jane said, "Is it true? Are you pregnant?"

"Yes Aunt Jane."

"Then you must not change to were form like I did or you will lose it. Promise me you will be careful and you will stay in human form."

"I promise I will do my best."

Jane released her breath in a huge gush, "That's all right then. Congratulations, I am happy for you and for all of us. Yours is the first of your generation's cubs. Beware one of the cousins. Felicia is still bitter about her losses."

"We hope it wont be the last cub born to us or to the pride."

Jane hugged her then and agreed.

Marcus smiled at the tableaux and said "Rosa, Jane you never cease to amaze me, Thank you, now could we please have breakfast?" His stomach rumbled agreement then and everyone laughed.

"Certainly I'll make omelets and toast and sausage for you all."

Chris waited until everyone who was still home had come to the table and she announced that she was expecting. Her news was greeted with applause by some and a sullen silence from one of her cousins, who excused herself and fled rather than join the others in celebration, Chris determined to find her later and talk out what was bothering her. The last thing the pride needed at this delicate time was an internal feud. The ISPS would be watching them closely to be sure they were the right choice to represent all the cats on the new world council. Marcus would be a wonderful voice of reason and would be excellent at delegating hunters for rogues and mutts. The Europeans were here to set up a branch council for the "New World" as they put it." Marcus did air quotes as he said new world."Everyone laughed.

The other cousin everyone was worried about actually took the news well and congratulated her on her pending birth. She asked whether they knew if it would be a boy or girl and so Chris explained that she was only eight weeks along. Her cousin Missy said, "I hope you are stronger than I was and avoid changing. But congratulations anyway and good luck." She lifted her orange juice in a salute. Others seeing it raised theirs as well and the toast for luck became general. The rest of breakfast was filled with good spirits and loads of advice on diet and exercise and suggestions on where to shop for clothes and baby items. It was altogether a genial meal. After breakfast the pride dispersed, going about their daily chores or to their jobs in town.

Chris set up her appointments with the midwife and the pride's OB Gyn specialist for her prenatal appointments.

CHAPTER 12

Chris' pregnancy went well for the first four months and then she started swelling in her feet and lower legs. Her OB Gyn doctor said, "OK it is bed rest for you my dear. We don't want this to cause any more difficulties."

"How long must I lay in bed?"

"The rest of your pregnancy. I suggest you learn a hobby like knitting and I hope you like to read and watch TV."

"Crap. Well I do like to read and I enjoy the occasional TV show. I guess I could learn a needle craft like knitting or crocheting. I have always been interested in watching the others embroider and such so maybe I could learn to do that."

"Whatever you choose will be fine as long as it keeps you in bed. Also I want you to have your feet and legs elevated for at least an hour

50

twice daily. They need to be higher than your heart. OK?”

“OK. Will will be worried and I expect the others will be too but as long as I am good my baby will be alright?”

“Should be fine. Now if you don’t have any more questions?”

“No I guess not except what about my showers?”

“A bath would be better but as long as you don’t spend an hour on your feet you should be OK. I recommend elevating your feet after you shower.”

“Good idea, I’ll do that.”

“OK you can call me any time but now I have rounds at the hospital so I will see you in a month.”

Chris left the office and stopped by the medical supply attached to the hospital where she picked up an inflatable cube to use when she had to have her legs above her heart. That done she went home and talked to Rosa about what the doctor had said. “So where should I do this I mean I don’t want to take up the bed.”

“That’s easy we will just put you and Will in a guest room with a king size bed. Come on and I’ll help you move your clothes and as for a hobby I can teach you how to crochet and one of the aunts can teach you about needle point embroidery. How will that be?”

51

"Thank you Rosa I don't want to be a bother."

"You are never a bother, unlike some I could mention." Then she laughed. "You know who I mean too."

"I have an idea." She laughed along with Rosa. The woman they were referring to was an elderly aunt who complained about everything. Things were either too soft or too hard or things were either too hot or too cold and similar complaints. But she had been a great hunter and so she was catered to. She decided she needed to entertain Chris during her enforced lie in.

She had great stories of the pride before Chris and Will were born. She remembered hunts and some were epic like the time they brought down a buffalo. And she loved sharing anecdotes about Marcus her son. Chris loved the stories. And she discovered a wit as sharp as a razor and not the bumbling old woman she had expected from the constant complaining they had all grown used to.

Aunt Anna, which was the name of the elderly woman, was a great raconteur. She told a story about when Marcus had grown and had caught his first rabbit. He was so proud until when he put it down it scampered away. Any peccadillo any of their parents had made were fodder for her stories and Chris and Will enjoyed them tremendously. Anna also taught Chris how to do needle work. They spent hours embroidering pillow cases and sheets, towels and a cover for the baby's bed.

The months seemed to drag by and it became increasingly difficult to fight the change. At one point Chris caught herself in a partial change that happened while she was sleeping. Will, aware of her as always, woke her before it could go very far so the baby was safe and so was she, but it was a close call and frightened her.

There was a baby shower and the women gave her a complete layette including christening clothes. Everything was in pale yellow or the softest green since she didn't know what she was having. Chris and Will both wanted it to be a surprise.

And then one night Chris woke to pain and the urge to go to the bathroom. Will woke instantly and realized she was in labor. He threw on clothes and hurried to find the midwife who lived in town. She was ready to go quickly and Will hurried her to the truck and the journey home. By the time they got home the labor was well advanced and Chris' baby was close to crowning.

"Alright now push."

"Breathe."

"Push again."

"Oh I was thinking about my mother." came his response. What about Eliza Jane or Jennifer Marie?" The midwife said mildly.

"Good idea Chris. What do you think?"

"Excellent. How about Jennifer Marie?"

"Do you want to call her Jennifer or Marie or Jenny Marie."

"Marie works for me Will, or Jenny Marie."

"I like Jenny Marie too."

"Now you know. Rosa, she is Jenny Marie."

"How lovely, I miss my sister too."

CHAPTER 13

"Watching you two reason things out was a real pleasure. If you do everything that way you will have a very happy marriage." Rosa dimpled a smile and Marcus said "I concur."

"We try to compromise with each other. But only if it doesn't involve ethics, then we don't need to compromise because we think alike."

"Yes and that is why you will make excellent leaders for our pride when we decide to step down and travel for our retirement. You will also take our places on the ISPS council."

"Are you sure?"

"Oh yes we have been waiting and will retire in a couple of years. That should give you enough time to become used to the decision making involved."

"I am surprised you don't give it to Charles or James."

"They agree with me that you would make a better ruler than they would, they are not strong enough. Their words not mine."

"I am flattered that you think I am worthy. Thank you. I wonder what Chris will say."

"You wonder what Chris will say about what? Hello Marcus, Rosa. Hello love." Chris came in to Marcus' office.

"What you will say about me taking over the control of the pride."

"Oh love that would be perfect you have all the qualities a leader should have."

"Marcus wants to give me control in two years when he and Rosa want to retire and travel. I think I might be ready by then. It will mean an early retirement from the USGS but then I will be taking over the bookstore."

"Well you are a grade eleven so you will have at least ten years service so half retirement. And I will still have my practice. We will be fine financially. And you know I will support all your decisions publicly although I may disagree in private."

"I expected nothing less from you my dear. I figure we can go on as we have been and compromise when necessary."

"Besides it is good practice for when our daughter is old enough to argue with us about rules." Chris grinned.

55

"She'll be good at arguing if she is anything like her mother." Will laughed at Chris' expression.

"Oh you!" was her rejoinder and then she laughed, "You're right. I should have been a lawyer!"

Marcus and Rosa joined in the banter and said, "You would never have lost a case if your past is anything to go by."

Chris laughed with them.

"You're right." She said giggling. "You are so right."

CHAPTER 14

The two years were up when Marcus gathered the pride together in his office to inform them he was stepping down as leader and that Will would be taking his place. He explained his reasoning and James and Charles told the others that they supported his choice. Then the pride was asked to vote to confirm Will's leadership. The vote was unanimous in favor and so the mantle of kingship passed to a new generation. Everyone congratulated him on his elevation and the pride dispersed. The women to prepare a feast to celebrate and the men to organize a hunt.

Marcus then called the sheriff, George and Henry to tell them about the change in leadership.

Their response was that his choice was expected and that they would be quite comfortable working with Will. The sheriff even went so far as to suggest that Will assume Marcus' seat on the ISPS council. Marcus told him that he had already informed the other members about the change including the Fey.

The bears were supportive and made suggestions as to how he could vote on the water project proposal. It would be the main order of business at the next meeting. Unless, of course it became necessary to hunt down a mutt or renegade. Then the water irrigation vote would be tabled for the following month. It was assumed that the proposal would pass to help the local farmers.

There was one thing that Will didn't know and it vexed him. Were they supposed to notify the Old World ISPS about the change or was it purely an internal matter? He also did not know how the Fey felt about his assention to the leadership of the were pumas or mountain lions, in the west. The New World International Society would have to pass on his membership for the cats just as the Old World Society had on Marcus. He would have to ask Marcus.

His opportunity came later that day. He was in the farm's office looking over the books when Marcus came in. "Say Marcus? How does my job now affect the old world ISPS? Do we need to tell them? Do they need to agree?"

"Oh I have already informed them that you are taking over the pride and the cats in the western US. I did not ask their permission. I did inform them and that is enough we are autonomous after all."

"OK, I just wondered if they had to agree with our decision."

"It is really none of their concern as long as the other council members agree to work with you they have no say in any decisions we make. Telling them was a courtesy and that's all."

"You made your point and I wont worry about it any more.

"Good there is something we do need to worry us. Zack just got off the phone with me and there is a bear that attacked a camper. At this point we are not sure if it is a were or an ordinary bear so we are treating it as though it is were. This is something you need to handle and believe me when I tell you that the others will be watching to see how you do. So don't fuck it up."

"Yes, sir. Do you want to join the hunt of the bear or do you want to leave it up to James and Charles and me and the women."

"I'll leave it up to you."
Will called James and Charles and the younger females to come to town and to meet them at the Fox and Hound, the staging area for the hunt. Then He joined the wolves and Zack, the new leader of the were bears at the club. He asked to be appraised of the situation and who knew of the

attack and how the bears are going to handle the hunt. "Well we bears are not sure at this point if it was a were or an ordinary bear cousin which killed the camper. I am hoping it was not one of ours but it is spring and after the winter we are all short tempered, it comes with being a bear."

"I understand that. How do we tell the difference in the attack?"

"A were will bite the neck and break the spine there. An ordinary bear is not so selective. And an ordinary bear will eat its kill without dismembering it whereas a were will dismember his kill. All we know at this point is that it was a bear kill. George, the sheriff is on his way in from the scene and he will tell us more when he gets here."

"I'll take a cup of coffee while we are waiting if you don't mind, Henry."

"Sure thing Will, coming right up."

They waited for awhile and the sheriff finally came in to deliver his assessment of the kill. "I am sorry to tell you Henry and Zack but it is a were kill the body was dismembered and the limbs were carefully arranged. Still at least we don't need to worry about any new attacks. He feasted well and there was very little meat left on the bones. He'll hole up and sleep now until he is hungry again so we have a couple of days to find him and shoot him."

Henry was past leader of the were bears. There were only he and his younger brother Zack and his sister in law and their twin cubs. The bears were essentially solitary or a family unit and their range was quite large so having another bear in their territory was an unpleasant surprise. They would be eager to see it destroyed and their name cleared. There were already rumors about the death circulating in the supernatural community.

As the sheriff was organizing the search grid one of the local fey came in and said breathlessly, "There is a bear marking territory on your range Henry. I thought you should know. He is a big grizzly and he doesn't act like any bear I have ever seen before. He acts more human somehow. And he marked my tree. He also deliberately sprayed his pee all over it after he clawed it." Then the dryad turned and they could see the claw marks on her back. These would echo the marks on her tree.

"I am sorry to see you have been attacked and I promise we will find this renegade and dispose of him."

"Thank you, that is all I ask."

"Where is your tree and how long ago did this happen?"

"Oh Sheriff it was around a half an hour ago and he was moving north toward the Rockys." He is in the Uncompahdres and he is huge."

"Thank you for your help Dryad,"

"We need to help each other as part of the secret world. We don't need humans to learn too much."

60

"True." The sheriff brought out a topographic map of the area and asked the dryad to show them where she had seen the bear and to show where he was moving. She was happy that they were going to destroy the renegade and was eager to help. She pointed out the bear's probable path given how he had approached her tree and the direction he had taken on leaving. The hunters paid close attention and the sheriff assigned areas on a grid for searching. Given how slow the bear was moving they should be able to find him soon. They all piled into jeeps and took off for the mountains and their hunt. They got there in good time by using logging roads. They parked near the site of the kill and the wolves and cats sniffed out the bears trail.

CHAPTER 15

The hunters spread out in their assigned pattern and began to follow Zack, Charles and Will as they lead the way with the wolves. Henry was in the lead with them when they found the first tracks which led to the kill. It was obvious that the bear had deliberately stalked the victim and Henry growled deep in his throat and chest. It was a more menacing sound than a roar would have been and his anger was clear as he snarled.

The hunters followed the tracks to the kill and saw what had spooked the people who had found the dead body. The limbs were arranged carefully arm leg, leg and arm side by side below the gutted torso. Obviously human intelligence was at work and that meant a renegade. The tracks away from the kill site were clear and easy to follow. Before long they found the entrance to the cave the were had selected to hole up in. They could hear him breathing and there was a liquidy sound in it. That could mean the were was sick, perhaps with pneumonia or something equally fatal without treatment.

There was a snuffling sound then and a roar followed as the bear came charging out to attack Henry.

There was a quick slash of claws and Henry was torn from shoulder to hip across his chest and upper stomach. The bear followed up with a series of strikes to Henry's face and torso taking him by surprise and then the cats were on him.

Marcus leaped on his back digging his claws into the were's shoulders and biting his neck. Meanwhile the sheriff and his wolves circled the bear keeping him off balance and springing in to snap at his hamstrings and ankles. Will caught one of the bears paws in his teeth and then ripped into the bears belly with his hind claws. He dropped away before the bear could claw him with his free paw. Two of the wolves transformed and aimed the rifles they had brought with them. As soon as Will had dropped away they fired and hit the bear squarely in the chest. The were bear dropped to all fours and shook his head. Roaring defiance he attempted to roll onto Marcus but Marcus jumped free and that left the bear in a vulnerable position. Henry transformed and shot. The bullet found its home in the bear's skull as the bear thrashed a little and then lay still. Henry collapsed then. Marcus and Will transformed. Will began first aid stopping the blood flow from Henry's chest and gut. The sheriff, George, dug into the pack he had been holding and found bandages and antiseptic. He also located the needles and sterile thread used for emergency suturing. Fortunately the wounds were not all that deep and simple stitches were enough. The wounds on Henry's face were another story and he had come very close to losing his left eye. Will wanted one of the EMTs to check his handiwork but none of them had come on the hunt so it would mean a trip to town while Henry stayed at the Fox and Hound.

The EMT who came in response to Will's call to the station said the only concern he had was with Henry's eye and he thought it looked as though his cornea had been scratched. So they put some antibiotic drops in it and placed a patch over the eye with instructions to see the ophthalmologist as soon as possible. The EMT suggested that he call for Henry and make the appointment for the following morning. Henry agreed.

63

So at eight AM Henry was in seeing the surgeon. The surgeon prescribed three different eye drops to help with the healing and recommended a patch for three days. He drops were administered twice daily and the patch replaced. The ophthalmologist saw Henry after the three days and pronounced the healing process well begun. She said the drops needed to be continued for three weeks but he could dispense with the patch. Henry was delighted.

His mate thought he looked rather rakish with the scar. She showed him how sexy she thought it was which made him feel young again. He and she decided to take a long trip and visit the western national parks like The Grand Canyon and Yosemite. So leaving the bears in Zack's capable paws they took their camper and started on their trip. They promised to keep in touch every evening while they were gone unless they were in a dead zone. And they couldn't find a land line to make the call. The trip was one they had been planning for a long time. Henry knew Zack was perfectly capable of leading the family.

CHAPTER 16

Zack kept Will in formed about the progress made by Henry and Sally and filled him in on their sense of wonder at what they saw. The couple were treating their trip as a second honeymoon.

Will then told him about their expected twins and how excited Marcus and Rosa were when they were told. They had decided to follow Henry's and Sally's example and go traveling to the North West. Their parents were thrilled with the idea of being grandparents again. Their daughter Jennifer Marie was excited to be able to babysit as she was twelve years old and wanting to earn pocket money. The pregnancy went well with none of the problems Chris had experienced with the Jenny. The twins were named after the flowers, Jasmine and Lavender.

Shortly after their birth James passed away and Chris and Will grieved his loss. At first they couldn't believe it. James had just been over at their house to play with the twins and to shoot hoops with their daughter and James favorite grand child, Jenny Marie two days before. Everyone was devastated. None more so than Marcus and Rosa. They came home from their wandering to celebrate his life.

By the time they arrived Will had moved on through the stages of grief to finally accepting the loss. The others were at various stages of grief and Chris was trying to stay together for Jenny Marie's sake. Jenny was convinced that had they not played basketball her favorite uncle would have not died. She was finding it very hard to accept the reality. Chris was able to help her in trying to deal

65

with her loss and they were making real progress
which relieved everyone who loved her. There was
a real concern that she might not pull out of her
depression and actually grieve. Fortunately she
was stronger than that and had moved through the
anger phase finally and on to guilt and bargaining.
She wanted things to go back to the way they had
been and she believed it was her fault that they
couldn't. Then she would feel depressed. She
seemed to be bouncing back and forth between
depression and the need to have things return to
what was normal before.

Chris was sure that she would move on to
accepting the reality of life without her uncle but it
was going to take time. Meanwhile she was
helping take care of the twins and they seemed to
help her regain her usually sunny disposition, at
least when she was around them. So Chris and
Will found reasons why they needed her to
babysit.

Then it became necessary. The ISPS was
holding a series of meetings at Purgatory Ski
Resort. Their choice was based on the fact it was
close to home for several of the members of the
council. The exceptions were the vampires and
some of the fey. The were bears, wolves and cats
were local and so were the dryads, nyads and the
fairies who lived in meadows in the mountains.
The elves, dwarfs and goblins lived further east as
did the orcs. The orcs were so few in number that
when they were represented their home emptied of

both if them. They would probably die off soon as the remaining orcs were male unless they were able to convince Asian or European orcs to move to the US. They would not be missed if they did pass on. Their personal habits were not condusive to making friends with other supernatural members such as the dryads. It was the smell!

CHAPTER 17

One of the main concerns for the supernatural community was the logging that was being allowed in part of the National Forest in the Rocky Mountains. The dryads were being decimated at an alarming rate since they were tied to their trees. They had already died off in the north west and in other areas. It didn't matter that the men doing the cutting were planting new trees. Without proper pollination and propagation new dryads could not be born.

It was known that there were few dryads in Europe but their logging practices were different than those in the States. Clear cutting was not usual there. In America it was not unusual. The dryads had called the emergency council meeting to discuss their plight.

It was decided that the dryads would be artificially pollinated and the resulting seeds would be taken to property owned by the other fey. That was the only solution they could think of. They knew it was a stopgap solution but at least it was better than the alternative. The dryads reluctantly agreed.

The next item on the agenda was the incursion of snowmobiles and hunters onto lands controlled by the wolves and the four wheelers used in hunting in the east. This was a new threat and they were petitioning the states to disallow the use of wheeled vehicles when hunting just like they had banned hunting from the roads. There would still be poachers who ignored the rules but they were fewer than might be expected. The wolves of Canada were particularly interested in this ruling. They used snow mobiles and four wheelers to get to the back country where they changed and hunted. The wolves in Yellowstone were more concerned about campers and hikers than they were hunters. The bears were all represented by Zack who was somewhat over whelmed by the whole process. But he soon got over his shyness and made his opinion known.

The last order of business was the use of irrigation canals and the way they were being tended. The main channels were being cleaned and looked after by a family of humans and there was some concern that they would see something they shouldn't. The water nymphs were concerned especially since they no longer could simply drown anyone who saw them.

The discussions went on for a few hours with no solutions in sight when Will suggested a recess until the next morning. Once that was agreed upon the delegates parted for their respective rooms and dinners.

Will and Chris talked over what had been discussed and she said she would think about possible solutions including the idea of buying up land next to the forest and planting fertilized dryad seeds there. Since it would be private land there would be no concern about logging. However that didn't help the dryads currently living in the areas being logged. The youngest could be transplanted but the older established trees could not. It was a problem to be considered carefully. One of the wolves had suggested sabotaging the logging equipment. That was voted down immediately by the dryads and the others. Then the elves had suggested magically transplanting the established trees onto the private land owned by them in the east.

This solution was greeted with gratitude by the dryad community. In the normal course of events they would have been laughed out of the meeting but these were not normal times. Humans were increasingly occupying land needed by the supernatural world and eventually Chris thought they would have to stop being hidden. But that held its own dangers. What if there was a bounty placed on them? No, better they remain hidden.

They may end up extinct but still it is better to become extinct while remaining hidden than to go public and be put on the run from bounty hunters. The vampires recommended staying hidden and the council voted agreement. The decision was to transport the youngest dryads to private lands and the elves said they would transport the mature trees to their forests in the east. Particularly they would go to their preserves in the Appalachian Mountains. As for the water nymphs it was suggested they change their waters for more open ways like the Red River, the Colorado and the Mississippi. Moving to the bayeaux of Louisiana was also the recommendation of the council.

The decision of the council was to limit hunts to private land and registered wilderness areas where the chance of being seen changing form was minimal. That concluded the current business and the last day of the meeting was spent socializing. The elves hosted a party in their suite and played music for the members. Elvish music was a thing not to be missed.

CHAPTER 18

The bears were particularly pleased with the results of the meeting and claimed they already hunted in the local wilderness area. The dryads were delighted with the elves and were already making suggestions about mentoring the elves' children. With the meeting ended on such a positive note Will and Chris invited the other council members to visit them on their ranch, in the Uncompahgres. The elves were delighted as they were wood elves and had never been in the area before.

The cats were delighted because they had never had dealings with the elves prior to the meeting. They planned a barbecue and dance to celebrate which made the elves happy. They were interested in the music of the indigenous people and this was a perfect way to hear it. The songs were hypnotic and moved their spirits. They in turn shared some of their music with the cats and one evening they went to the Fox and Hound and played for all the patrons there. They received a warm welcome and were the objects of covert curiosity but they soon won over the weres who were present. Their music was given standing ovations which they found particularly gratifying. After three days with the cats they went home to the Appalachians with tales about the mountain lions hospitality and how gracious they were. They also had stories about how cute the twins were and how lovely Jenny was.

They invited Will and Chris and their children to come East to visit during the following summer. Chris accepted for all of them and then the cats waved good bye to their charming guests with promises to keep in touch. They were surprised by Jenny's reaction to the elves. She had become suddenly shy especially when one of the young males was present and Chris noticed. She decided to keep a close watch on her daughter and the young prince. She had to admit he was amazingly handsome with dimples when he smiled which was often. It was obvious that Jenny was experiencing her first crush.

Of course cross species mating occurred occasionally but was usually short lived as no offspring were possible. Still under Chris' watch they did not act on the attraction, especially since the elf in question was much older than Jenny and was aware of the girl's attachment. He made sure they were never alone together and Chris' estimation rose as a result. She thought about mentioning the one-sided affair to Will but decided that it would be a waste of time. To Will, Jenny was still a little girl so he would say Chris was imagining things.

Jenny moped for a couple of weeks following the elves' departure but then her usually happy disposition reemerged and Chris thought she had forgotten about the elf.

CHAPTER 19

One morning when Jenny didn't come in for breakfast Chris went to her room to discover her bed not slept in and no sign of her. Her backpack was missing as were some of her clothes and Chris had a sinking feeling that she knew where the fourteen year old had gone. The next thing she did was check the household money and found most of it missing. Her fears were justified. She told Will what she suspected and he had a hard time believing it. Chris said "We need to call the elves and let them know that we believe Jenny is on her way to them."

"How does she even know where to go? The Appalachian Mountains are a huge chain. If that young elf is responsible for this I will kill him."

Chris was shocked to the bone, "You will do no such thing. I tried to tell you that Jenny had developed a crush but you persisted in thinking she was too young. You forgot our love and how young we were when we knew we loved each other, so you will do no such thing."

"But..."

"But nothing! That young man knew about Jenny's feelings and he made sure they were never alone together, or didn't you notice that either?"

"But..."

"Ooh, men! I swear you are all dense! Unless you are hit over the head with reality you live in your own world."

"But how did you know about it?"

"Obviously it is because I am rooted in the real world not my imagination."

"Oh now that's not fair. Jenny is still a child."

"No, Will, Jenny is a young woman and has been one for three years. You are lucky she didn't decide to fall for one of her cousins from the Sangre de Christos. Now will you call the elves or shall I?"

"You are sure he didn't encourage her?"

"Positive."

Will moved into his office and made the call. It was awkward. But he finally got his point across when the elf king said "If he has encouraged her in anyway he will be very sorry!"

Will told him what Chris had said about his behavior and received a grunt in response. Then the elf said, "It is well. We will watch for her."

"We will be tracking her from this end too."

"We will find her between us."

CHAPTER 20

Jenny Marie jogged toward Durango and the bus station where she would catch her ride to Bristol, Virginia. At least that was her plan. She had no idea how she would manage if it wasn't a direct trip from Denver. Best to cross that bridge if she came to it.

She stopped for breakfast in Durango where she was shocked by the prices of a cup of coffee and toast. She hoped her funds would last long enough to get her to the Blue Ridge Mountains and the object of her heart's desire.

She learned her trip was going to involve several changeovers from one bus to another and she was nervous suddenly. *What if she missed one of her connections? What did she do then? Well no point in worrying about it until it happened.* She hurried her steps to the station. Her bus would be leaving in about ten minutes.

She was the first one aboard and because it was early in the day there were not too many people going to Denver. She settled in her seat and put her backpack on the seat beside her. That kept anyone from sitting next to her. She knew that there were human predators who rode buses looking for victims and she was determined not to become one.

The bus would be stopping in Oklahoma for lunch and then in Missouri for dinner and a changeover. From there they would travel to Nashville and another stop. Nashville was her last bus change and she would board the bus for Bristol Virginia. From Bristol she would hike north until she found the elves. At least that was her plan.

It happened in Nashville. She got off the bus and a man approached her to ask if she needed a ride to her hotel. "No, I'm not staying."

"Honey, a young girl like you shouldn't be traveling alone. Why don't you let me help you? There are bad people out there who would hurt a little girl like you." He reached for her backpack.

Jenny jerked it out of his grasp. "Leave me alone."

"Honey, don't be like that I am just trying to help you." He reached for the pack again.

Softly she said, "Back off or pay for it. I will cut you." She had extended one of her hands

and poked the back of his hand with a sharp claw
which she immediately retracted.

He jerked his hand back and with a muffled
oath sucked at the wound she had made. "What the
fuck did you cut me with you little bitch?"

"My nails. Now leave me alone." Jenny
was shaking inside. That had been too close.
Would he leave or try to get retribution?

He moved off then, swearing the whole
time. Then he saw a young man who looked lost
and he approached him, Jenny forgotten. They
spoke a while. Then the boy gave him a tattered
backpack and they left together. Jenny felt sorry
for the boy, who looked about sixteen. He was
either naive or really stupid. Even at fourteen she
knew not to trust in strangers, especially ones like
the man. He had looked fair but felt slimy.

Breakfast was over and it was time to board
the bus for the last leg of her journey among
people. Jenny couldn't wait. She had currently
been awake for twenty four hours and she was
beginning to feel enervated. The excitement of
seeing her prince charming could only carry her so
far. She decided to get a hotel room in Bristol if
she had enough money. All she had left was
seventy five dollars of the five hundred she had
started with. Meals had cost more than she had
been prepared for. She boarded the bus and settled
in the seat behind the driver with her pack beside
her. She had managed to sit right behind him on
each connection. She had the idea it would be safer

when she saw some of the people who rode the buses. The smell from some of them was nauseating. And she itched when she thought about what sorts of bugs they might be carrying.

She dozed on this last ride and only woke when the bus stopped at a traffic light or went over railroad tracks. When the driver finally pulled in to the station in Bristol she was sleeping soundly. It took some effort for the driver to wake her but eventually he did. Jenny was embarrassed and flushed an unbecoming red. "Oh, I am so sorry."

"Its alright Miss. It happens all the time."

"Well thank you for waking me. Can you recommend a motel not too far away that is cheap and clean?"

"Sure, Go down three blocks and turn right and you'll see a Motel Six. My cousin runs it so I know it's clean. Rooms are sixty five bucks for a poolside room. And forty five for the others. Good luck to you." He exited the bus then and waited by the open door. He would lock up when she was gone.

"Well good bye and thank you!"

He chuckled, "You're welcome. Good bye youngster. Oh and she provides a Continental Breakfast, coffee and pastry, in the lobby starting at six AM."

"Thanks again." Jenny jogged to the designated place and found the motel. She paid her forty five and got the key. The first thing she did was take a shower using the shampoo and soap provided. The hot water felt wonderful after a day and a half riding on the bus. She turned on the Television and collapsed onto the bed. She was asleep before she could change the channel.

CHAPTER 21

Meanwhile her family was busy tracking her. First they had gone to the airport to see if she had flown out to Virginia. When they drew a blank they went to the local bus station. No luck there either. Then Will had the idea that maybe she had gone to Durango for her ride. He struck gold. By the time they discovered how she was getting to Virginia she was getting her change over in Tennessee. They decided to drive straight through to Bristol with the hope they could catch her before any harm was done.

They arrived in Bristol and sought out the bus station. They missed seeing Jenny by minutes. While she was checking in to the motel they were questioning the station master about her. He in turn told them that she had talked to her driver and had brushed off a man and he didn't know anything else. They found the driver in the lounge area for personnel and asked him about her. Once they showed him her picture he was willing to tell them where she was.

They arrived at the Motel Six as Jenny was finishing her shower. The woman at the desk was reluctant to give them any information until Will showed her Jenny's picture, the one he carried in his wallet. Then she told them her room number and said she hoped that there were no problems from a legal standpoint.

Will reassured her that they just wanted their daughter to come home and that he was sorry if he had sounded irate. He said, "I am not angry with you. You were taking care of business. I am frustrated with my daughter and her over reaction to her first crush."

"Oh you poor man. No wonder you are upset. Have some coffee and calm yourself. I know what teenage girls are like and if you let her see how angry you are you will alienate her. You can let her see that you were worried about her, that you love her and that you are proud of her for her resourcefulness. Then you can tell her you wish she had talked her decision over with you first."

"She knows we love her." Will said somewhat defensively.

"I don't doubt it but she still needs to hear it. Take it from me. I have been through something very similar to what you are experiencing. Young girls can be extremely headstrong especially when you try to prove them wrong. My daughter..." Her voice trailed off. Then she shook her head and said briskly, "All you can do is be supportive when she discovers that her affections are not returned."

By this time Jenny was asleep and dreaming of her prince.

The innkeeper gave Will the extra key to Jenny's room and wished him luck. He and Marcus went upstairs to Jenny's door. He thought about just going in but decided to knock first. It was a good thing he did because Jenny's dreams had turned dark and involved the man from the bus depot. The knocking woke her from her nightmare and she said come in before she realized she wasn't home. She was so relieved to see her dad and granduncle and not the man in her nightmare she ran to them and cried. "Oh daddy. I am sorry." She sniffled, "How did you find me?"

"We asked at the airport and the bus station and they remembered you. We drove here and traced you by asking your driver if he had seen where you went. Then he told us about his cousin and the motel. You make friends wherever you go my dear." He hugged her tight. "Now what frightened you?"

"Oh daddy there was this horrible man who tried to make me go with him. I stabbed his hand and he let me go. He felt so slimy but his words were nice. Like he wanted to keep me safe. But there was something that felt wrong. My gut said run away."

"I am glad you are safe. I am proud of you for standing up to that creep although I am frustrated that you put yourself in such a position in the first place. In any case you didn't know it but we were planning to come visit the wood elves this summer anyway."

"I had no idea! How come no one told me?"

"It was to be a surprise. The wood elves invited us to come for the summer solstice and your mother and I thought it would be fun to surprise you and the twins."

"Did I spoil going?"

"Not at all. I will let them know we found you as they were concerned."

"I really made a mess of things didn't I?"

"No dear girl, but it could have been us finding your dead body. Please don't do anything like this again."

"I promise Daddy!"

Will called the wood elves and Chris to let them know everything was fine and she was safe. They were all happy with the news. Chris asked to speak with Jenny Marie and Will gave her the phone. What Chris said to Jenny was never mentioned but it did the trick and Jenny never did anything that stupid again. In fact eventually she became enamored with a very handsome cousin. This cousin was only two years older than her and was extremely honorable and trustworthy. He was large for a mountain cat but very gentle and a gentleman in the Southern traditional sense of the word.

CHAPTER 22

Chris had introduced Jenny to one of her cousins from the Sangre de Christos range and she had promptly fallen for him. They enjoyed many of the same things so when they went to spend solstice with the elves Jenny had no problem with her prince's engagement to a northern elf.

She and the others enjoyed their time in the Blue Ridge with the elves. The night of the solstice the elves arranged a hunt with an elf accompanying each cat, They were fascinated by the concerted way in which the cats surrounded the herd of white tailed deer and they were impressed when the cats took out a sick doe and an injured buck adding to the welfare of the herd. The elves had not expected such conservation on the part of the cats.

The elves also held a dance to honor the solstice and their guests. The dance was held in a meadow deep in the mountains. Delicate flower scented breeze drifted among the dancers. Moonlight and lanterns illuminated the fairy tale scene.

Jenny was politely distant to the prince when she declined to dance with him which surprised them both. Then she decided it was due to embarrassment over her earlier escapade. She sought him out to apologize and he graciously accepted. He told her then that he hoped they could work together in the future and she agreed. They were guarded with each other until the prince saw her with her cousin. Then he found he warmed considerably. He knew that he need have no concerns for her heart. She was obviously in love and so was the young man. She danced almost exclusively with him.

There were specialty dances like Jigs brought from Ireland and western Europe which everyone enjoyed watching. The food was an interesting blend of dishes with each of the participating elves supplying a family favorite. For drink there was clear spring water cold from its journey underground.

The solstice party was a huge success and Chris decided that they should do something similar when they were home.

The dryads supplied dead wood for a bonfire and the female elves jumped the blaze before it got very large. The youngest elves tried their hands at toasting marshmallows which made for some sticky faces and hands. When the dancing became general again Jenny Marie finally danced with the prince and the king smiled knowing that a break with the cats would not occur.

They were invited to return for the winter solstice when the prince and princess would marry. Will declined graciously as the cats had special celebrations during the period. But he decided to send a gift as that was a traditional act.

Jenny and her lion prince grew ever closer and eventually the inevitable occurred and she found out she was pregnant. "Oh Richard, what will we do? By the time we will be married I will be showing a lot and they will be so disappointed in me."

"Do you want to have the baby?"

"Of course! How can you ask such a question?"

"There will be plenty of time for babies after we are married so if you wanted to abort this one I would understand."

"No and if I have to have it by myself I will." She said with heat. Angry tears scalded her cheeks.

"You will never have to have a child without me." Richard said firmly. He held her then, "I love you. You are dearer to me than anyone else could ever be." He kissed her tenderly and she relented.

Thus their wedding was by elopement during the time her mother Chris was planning the wedding. The day it was discovered that they were gone was the day she was to go for the first fitting of her wedding gown and to taste cake samples. There were still four months to go before the nuptials and Chris was torn between gratitude and frustration at missing a mother's prerogative.

The couple stayed gone for a year although they did stay in touch with their moms and dads,

"Hello?"

"Hi dad."

"How are you two?"

"We are three now, grandpa. You have a grandson. We named him Marcus James."

"Congratulations! Here let me put you on speaker and you can repeat that." Will laughed. "OK go ahead."

"You are the grandparents of a baby boy we are naming Marcus James."

"He will be so proud to hear it."

"Yes not everyday does someone become a great grandpa. Your sisters are getting married next summer. Can you make it home for the wedding?"

"We are on our way home now and should be there in about a week. Jenny wants to have our son christened at home so you and my folks can be there."

"Where are you now?"

"Maine near New Hampshire. We spent the summer at Martha's Vineyard. And then came here to see the fall colors."

"It is beautiful! Hi dad."

"Hi Jenny. Congratulations on your successful pregnancy."

"Thank you. You will not believe how fast he is growing. He is already crawling and by the time we get home I expect he will be trying to walk."

"How old is he?"

Jenny blurted the truth before she could think about it, "Six months."She realized what she had said and her eyes went wide and she put a fist to her mouth. "We didn't mention it sooner because I was afraid you would be disappointed in me for not waiting until we were married."

"Oh my dear, your mother and I didn't wait either. I am so sorry you were afraid of how we would react."This from Will as Chris said, "Dears, we are happy that you are together and love each other and I never want you to worry about how we will react to you again. I couldn't be happier for you. Do you want to have a hunt to celebrate? Or would you prefer a party?"

"A family hunt would be perfect."

"OK a hunt it will be."

"We are heading into the New Hampshire mountains now and I am not sure about reception so if we get disconnected, we love you and will check in every night until we are home."

"Jenny?" They got static in reply. Then they heard, "Mom...you...re?

"We're here!"

"We...lost...m."

The signal went silent and Will realized that they had hung up. "They will check in when they stop for the night."

"Yes. Oh Will what wonderful news. I wanted to be a grandma."Chris laughed. "Wait until we tell the twins they are aunties."

"They will be thrilled and they will want to babysit."

"Yes and it will be good practice for them for later when they have their own children."

The week went by and Jenny and Richard made it home in time for Sunday brunch. Everyone cooed over the baby and they all commented on how handsome he was. They also mentioned how well behaved he was which led to stories about Jenny and Richard when they were little.

"Remember when Jenny decided to decorate the furniture by writing on it with a finish nail?"

"Ooh yes I do! I was so frustrated and angry with myself for leaving them where she could reach them."

Jenny laughed at her mother's chagrin. "I remember that you yelled at me and put me in the corner for the time it took you to re-stain the scratches and how hard I cried. All because you yelled at me. But I never did it again."

Richard said, "Let's not mention our peccadilloes to Marcus. We don't need to give him ideas." Everyone laughed. "Well I remember painting a Navajo rug with your oil paints. That and the dresser and the spread on the bed where I was supposed to be having a nap."

"We had to get mineral spirits to remove the paint from everything. We never did get all of it out of that rug."

"I remember how upset Jenny was when she spent an afternoon making and decorating mud pies and you wouldn't try one." Chris said to Will.

"Oh I remember that!" Chris said. "I couldn't understand it since I had no problem eating ant dirt."

"I remember that but you only did it once."

"True."

"Well I think I hear a certain young man calling for momma so I would guess he is hungry."

"Yep, its about that time."

"Ooh can we feed him? Please?" The twins asked plaintively.

"Sure, his dinner needs to be warmed in the microwave so if you will come with me I will show you the timing." Jen excused herself and took the twins with her.

Chris said to Richard, "I feel as though I missed an important part of being a mother because I didn't get to plan my daughter's wedding so I would like you two to renew your vows here with the community as witness. I want to do the whole thing with the cake and vows and flowers and all."

"I'll talk to Jen. I am sure she will be willing to do that. The twins can be flower girls."

"And her father can give her away."

"Oh definitely."

"I think helping plan her wedding will be just what she needs. She hasn't been herself since Marcus James was born. Not enough sleep is my thought."

"Don't you help with him?"

"Yes but I don't hear him at night and she does. I thought about having her go to bed right after supper and that way she can get some sleep and I can interact with my son."

"That is a great idea. I suggest you do it."

"OK I will. Now though I need to find our lists of guests from before. You wouldn't happen to know if they still exist and where they are?"

"Actually I do, Richard, they are in the office in the file cabinet under wedding."

"Thank you for keeping them."

"Oh I keep all sorts of things like old school papers you both have written and report cards from when you were in school."

"How amazing!"

"Yes. Well I don't think you need to mention that last bit to anyone."

"Of course. Although Jen might want to see them."

"Well she wont if you don't tell her they exist. Now about the wedding?"

"Yes, I think she will be happy to know we are doing it and I will be sure she is the main focus of all the planning."

"Thank you Momma Chris. If she gets to help plan it I know her spirits will improve."

"You know she could be suffering from postpartum depression. She may need to feel desirable and be the center of attention for a while. This wedding could be just the ticket to bringing her out of it. Every woman needs to feel beautiful and desirable sometimes just like you men."

"Huh. I didn't think of that. All the attention is going to Marcus James and she may just feel like a milk cow or something."

"Exactly. Sooo...what will you do about it?"

"I need to find a babysitter for a Friday night so I can take her out dancing at the Fox and Hound. I haven't taken her out since well before he was born. It has been months."

"Then I would love to babysit for you as would your mother, the cousins and the twins."

"Thank you Chris. I am glad you were here to talk to."

"Think nothing of it dear boy. Now why don't you go get the guest lists? And we can start preparing invitations for the wedding."

Richard exited the room and moved to the office where he found the files she had told him about. Curiosity got the best of him and he started looking for the school report cards, There was a file marked Jen's School and he couldn't resist the urge to see what her school work had been like. "Wow!" She had mostly A's with a few B's in Math. He had known his wife was smart but not brilliant. He found a report that placed her IQ at one hundred seventy. It matched his and he thought that might mean their son would be bright in school too. Time would tell but he had little doubt since his son was already crawling and turning over. He had been able to lift and turn his head since he was a few days old. He also appeared to recognize Jen and him when they were in his view because he would smile and gurgle at them. *Enough thinking I need to get the list for Jen and tell her about my conversation with her mom. She will be excited I hope. Seeing her down the past month is eating me alive. I want my wife back.* Not many minutes had passed when Richard shook himself out of his funk and grabbed the list. It was time to take his wife out for a walk while Chris watched their sleeping son. This walk was important and he planned to ask Jen to marry him again just like the first time.

CHAPTER 23

They enjoyed the time alone and when Richard went down on one knee and asked Jen to marry him again at first she demurred then she laughed and said "Yes."

He then said that he felt that she had been short changed by not getting to have a big wedding and that Chris wanted to be a proper mother of the bride. Jen wasn't sure about it until he told her how hurt Chris had been by their elopement. She allowed that, "It might be fun at that to plan a wedding with a dinner and a reception and all."

Richard told her that Chris had kept the original guest list when she asked, "But who do we invite?"

"Oh how wonderful. Hopefully no one has moved or if they have that they put in a change of address at the post office." Her eyes sparkled in a way he hadn't seen in a few months. He knew then that Chris had the perfect idea to catch her interest. Then he asked her if she would like to go out Friday night for a date night and she giggled and said yes. Another good suggestion. He was glad he had talked to Chris about Jen.

Friday rolled around and Jen spent time on her appearance. She put on makeup which she hadn't done since before Marcus was born. She used a curling iron on her usually unruly hair and took extra care dressing. She wore a pair of cream cashmere slacks and matching sweater with embroidered and sequined autumn leaves on the right shoulder and arm.

Richard also took extra care with his appearance and wore a suit with a tie. He shaved extra close and was pleased with the result. He went to the living room to await Jen. He wanted her to know that he felt she was worth dressing up for.

He whistled when she came into find him. The cashmere clung to her hourglass figure. She looked beautiful. Richard was inclined to take her to bed and the hell with the dinner, movie and dancing but he knew she had counted on going out so he stood and offered her his arm. He was also painfully aware of his erection and decided that he would definitely be taking Jen to bed at the end of the evening.

Jen glowed at the obvious admiration in Richard's eyes and at his smile. Then he had whistled and she blushed. She was almost tempted to suggest a motel rather than dinner and the movie but she decided that since he had gone to so much trouble the least she could do was follow through on the date. Richard drove them to The French restaurant and their delicious dinner.

They started with white wine and escargot and then on to Baked Onion Soup then their fillet mignon and a classic red wine, a Cabernet. Desert was pastries from a tray of petit fours. They finished with brandy and coffee. Then it was time for the movie and Richard left tips for the waiter and the chef. They left the restaurant arm in arm and walked up the street to the theater. Jen was happier than she had felt in what seemed like forever. The movie was Romeo and Juliet with Leonardo De Caprio as Romeo. They loved it! Jen cried when the couple died and Richard comforted her which led to kisses which led to them going to the nearest hotel rather than dancing. Richard worshiped her with his body and she reciprocated. They flew and it was like the first time for them all over again. They made it home at dawn and found Chris in the kitchen with Marcus James. She poured them each a cup of coffee and with a sly grin asked how the movie was. Jen told her all about it and said she should talk Will into taking her to see it. Chris allowed that although Leonardo wasn't one of her favorite actors she did enjoy Shakespeare and liked Romeo and Juliet. They chatted for a while and then Jen yawned and confessed that they hadn't been to sleep yet. Chris chased them off to bed and told them that she would take care of MJ for the rest of the day. Marcus James, MJ giggled then and said what sounded like bye bye along with some coos and goo's. Everyone laughed and Jen and Richard kissed their son and Chris, Jen's mom, and headed for bed to catch up on a little of their missed sleep.

CHAPTER 24

Meanwhile one of the cousins had gone into town and then decided to go for a run in the park. She left her car in the parking lot and started on the trail. Her sneakers made little sound as she ran along the track that wended down by the river. She was surprised to have the park to herself but then decided that it was due to the early hour. The sun had barely cleared the mountains in the east as she stopped to drink from the clear stream of waters that fed the river. She never heard the man who came up behind her and struck her unconscious. The next thing she was aware of was that she was bound and naked and she couldn't change because of the way she was trussed. Jeanette was frightened for the first time in her life.

Chris wondered where she was when she didn't come home for breakfast but then she forgot about it with the preparations for Jen's wedding. Today was Jen's second fitting for her wedding dress and they would be tasting cakes later. When she thought about it later and the cousin, Jeanette, didn't show up for dinner either she became concerned and called the police. George answered the phone on the second ring.

"Police department."

"Hello George. It's Chris."

"Hey Chris what can I do for you?"

"George, I'm worried about Jeanette. No one has seen her today since she left for town early this morning. She is always home in time for dinner and she is still not here and it is Nine o'clock."

"Legally I can't really do anything about it until she has been missing for twenty four hours but I can suggest that my deputies keep a look out for her car. How is that?"

"It will have to do. Thanks George. Let me know if they find anything."

"Of course."

A couple of hours later the phone rang and when Will answered it George told him they had found Jeanette's car in the park parking lot and that it was locked and her purse was in it as was her phone. Her tracks had been followed to the spot where the underground spring fed the river and there they were lost in an odd odor there that smelled like Clorox. The trail ended with tracks from a four wheeler. George went on to say that the department was treating it as a missing person/ probable kidnapping case and that they had contacted mountain rescue and they were organizing search parties for the surrounding terrain.

Three days later a pair of hikers found the horrific remains of a woman under some brush and cardboard. The body had been mutilated postmortem.

The finger tips had been removed and the face was so disfigured that identification was only possible through DNA. Her teeth had been removed so dental records could not be consulted. Whoever had killed her had done so before because a first timer would not generally have been so meticulous. George called the FBI and requested the assistance of a profiler. He was convinced that he was looking at the work of a serial killer. Jeanette had been sexually assaulted premortem and postmortem and she had obviously been tortured. Both before and after her death. Will came to identify her body which was only possible by her tattoos. Will was shaken by what she had obviously gone through and decided that she would be cremated. No way would anyone else see her pitiful remains. He also promised George that he would help in the investigation in any way possible. He did not promise not to seek vengeance nor did George ask for it.

He did tell Chris that she was hard to identify and that she had been badly mistreated but that was all he would say. That night he had a nightmare about what he had seen. Chris held him while he shook and cried therefore Chris was determined that anything that could affect Will that profoundly had to be bad. She decided that none of the pride would be doing anything away from home alone such as running or shopping. Either two or three went together or it wasn't done.

The following week after the funeral one of the wolves went missing and again their vehicle was found abandoned with the wolf's purse and phone locked inside. This time there was a witness to the abduction. The dryad had gone to visit her mother and it was on her way home that she came upon two human men forcing the young female wolf into the trunk of their car. She was unconscious and had been trussed like a calf, hands and feet together making it impossible for her to change. She could not see the men's faces but she was able to describe the car and give George part of the license plate number. George put out an All Points Bulletin, an APB, for the dark colored Toyota or perhaps Honda and waited for it to bear fruit. Three days later the wolf's body was discovered on the edge of the park in a highly wooded area. The young female had been treated the same way as the cat had been.

George had gotten a list of dark Honda and Toyota registrations with the first letter as D on the license plate. There were several hundred and George set about the grueling task of eliminating suspects. He automatically eliminated any owned by women and the elderly.

What he and Will found most disturbing was that the victims were all members of the were community. When the third member came up missing and was a bear They were sure that the killers were somehow privy to the were community and they were worried for other supernaturals. A dryad was the next person to go missing and was only understood to be a victim when her tree suddenly burst into flame with no outside cause. It was time to call an emergency meeting of the ISPS.

The meeting was scheduled for the following weekend in Kansas City. The entire supernatural community sent representatives except for the orcs since there was only one of them left. It was decided that the goblins would represent the orc and would tell him what had been decided.

The members registered at a campground outside Kansas City and came in a variety of campers and brought several types of tents. The meetings were to be held at the camp ground's central pavilion and the first order of business was who could work together to catch and destroy the killers. Thanks to the dryads they had a description of the vehicle and that the humans were white males in their thirties with dark hair. They were average build which made identification more difficult.

The European ISPS sent them word that the same sort of thing was happening there and that it seemed to be well organized. Now the question was who were these organized murderers. Were they part of an anti supernatural group? What was their purpose in the torture and postmortem mutilation? It was time to fortify their holdings and to keep to groups of two or more.

George knew the head of a vampire run security company and he called him in. Zack and Will met him when he got off his private jet. He had flown in from New Orleans where he had a branch office.

CHAPTER 25

"Manuel Ortega van de Reinhardt? I am Will Deleon and this is..."

"Zack." Manuel smiled and shook hands with them. "Shall we go out to the ranch or did you want to meet here on the jet or in town?"

"I suggest we go to the ranch where we have privacy and security."

"I agree." Zack said in his gravely voice. "We know we can be safe there. I am surprised your wife is not with you."

"She is coming by car and should be here by nightfall. She left the day before me. I will leave her directions to the ranch here at the jet. If you would be so good as to give them to me?"

"Certainly Mr. Reinhardt." Will wrote out detailed directions for Beth. "If you are ready to go?"

Manuel grabbed his suitcase and briefcase and said. "Ready. And please call me Manuel."

"Yes sir. I will tell him that and when your wife gets here I will give her the directions to the ranch."

"Good, man. Thank you. After that if you want to stay in town I will cover your stay at the local B and B or if you would rather go to Purgatory Ski Resort I will cover that as well. Here's a hundred for the cab fare to which ever you choose."

"Thank you sir the ski resort sounds perfect."

"Have fun." And with that Manuel followed Will and Zack to Will's Jeep and the trip to the ranch. An hour later they pulled up in front of the house and Manuel grinned. "I like your home, Will. It reminds me of Spain and parts of Mexico and California."

"Thank you. We find it comfortable."

It was still barely afternoon when the Mercedes pulled up in front of the house and Beth got out. One of the cousins had been watching for her and opened the door before she could knock.

"Why thank you for your welcome. Is my husband here?"

Will and Manuel came hurriedly down the hall toward Beth. "Hello Love. You made good time. This is Will and the king of the pride."

"Good evening your majesty."

"Oh please call me Will. I do not stand on formality here Mrs. van de Reinhardt."

"Will it is then and please call me Beth."

"Beth, my wife Chris will be home soon. She went to town with one of the cousins. They will be here in time for tea."

"Oh lovely. I wasn't sure if you did tea and I have to admit to being hungry. Manuel? Have you tried Antelope yet? I recommend them. I had one this morning. Their blood has a unique almost smokey flavor." Beth said to her husband. "He will be a little weak for a day but he'll be fine." Beth added because she caught the look of shock on Louise's face. The woman smiled slightly then and excused herself.

When she was gone Beth laughed, "I thought you all knew I am a vampire too. I didn't mean to shock her."

"Oh I wouldn't worry about Louise she is rather over dramatic and no one pays her much attention because of it."

"Oh I am glad I didn't cause any trouble." She noticed a woman with an hourglass figure coming down the hall, who hurried when she saw the strangers in her entrance way.

"Ah, here is Chris my wonderful wife. Chris this is Manuel and Elizabeth van de

Reinhardt. They are the vampire delegates I told you about and will be helping us with our serial killers."

"I am so pleased to meet you. I thought I'd order tea a little early so we can relax and get to know each other while we have it. Now Mrs. van de Reinhardt, if you would like to freshen up?" Chris gestured for Beth to join her.

"That would be lovely. And please call me Beth."

"Certainly, Beth. I'll show you to your rooms."

"Thank you. I love your beautiful house. It feels as though it grew out of the mountains after the plans migrated from Spain."

"Thank you. In a way it did as it is made of adobe and local sandstone. It has been in the family for a couple of centuries. The ranch has been here since the Spaniards came up from Mexico."

"Well it is gorgeous." Beth smiled, "I hope when this is over that you and your husband can come visit us at Briarly and we can arrange a hunt for you. We have a herd of white tail deer that live on our farm."

"That would be very nice. Here is your suite. Your bathroom is through that door." Chris gestured toward a door in the south wall opposite the bed. She went to the phone and called the kitchen to request early tea while Beth went to the bathroom. A few minutes later Beth came out to examine the quilt on the bed and to put away the clothes in the closet and dresser. Chris offered to help but there wasn't a lot so Beth demurred. Within a few minutes her clothes were all put away and she turned to Chris and asked if they dressed for dinner or if her jeans would be OK.

"Jeans are perfect. We are an informal lot here."

"Oh good, because I only brought one dressy dress." She laughed and Chris joined her. They made their way back down the hall and found the men in the dining room where Louise had set up the tea service. There was tea, and coffee, along with cucumber sandwiches and fried pickles and other goodies suitable for high tea.

Tea concluded Beth and Manuel asked for details about the kills. George had been reticent about what had occurred when he reported to the council. He had given the bare bones and Beth and Manuel needed the details to flesh out the description. It could help them find and kill the murderers.

Will told Manuel and Beth everything he knew and then Manuel excused himself to go get his briefcase. It was where the details from his operative's report on the Darkness Hunters of the Van Helsing Society was. "I think you will find that their hate mongering and the descriptions of what they think ought to be done to all supernatural creatures to be telling." He gave a copy of the report to Will. "If you turn to page seven you will see what I mean."

Page seven gave in detail by disgusting detail a description of the torture and postmortem mutilations that had been done to the weres and the dryad. Chris started reading over Will's shoulder and became nauseous the more she read. She looked at her husband. "Is this what you saw?"

"Yes."he replied softly. "I was nearly physically sick. Reading about it is not nearly as bad as seeing the reality. But it is the same in every detail."

"Oh my god! We have to stop them."

"That is why we are here."

"What can I do to help?"Chris asked.

Beth said, "I am going to be bait. They don't know about vampires being out here and I can pretend to be a were and be seen with you and others for a few days. Then I will go for a run by myself in the park in town. Since that is where they are hunting. They will be surprised. We will take them out with your help. They will not be ready for a vampire you see. Restraints for us would be different than for a were. They would need titanium logging chain to restrain us."

"I will be within hailing distance of Beth at all times and you will be with me. They wont get away. Also I don't think we need to tell Zack or George about our plans to kill the murderers. They represent the law and would feel compelled to arrest them. That is not in my plans."

"No more is it in mine. If Henry was here I would bring him in but he and June are off camping in the Tetons on Pilgrim Creek. Dinner will be in about three hours if you are OK till then I suggest we rest a bit."

"Good idea, although I'm not sure rest is what I would call it!" Everyone laughed and Chris smacked Will's arm.

"Oh you! You will give our guests a bad impression of us."

"I wouldn't worry about it. We are rather hedonistic too." Beth said.

"Thank you for being understanding."

Beth giggled, "You're welcome. Can someone lead us back to our en suite."

"Be happy to." Will said.

CHAPTER 26

Beth played her part well and soon enough the cats forgot she wasn't one of them. It took about two weeks for her to blend in so well. It was also approaching the time for her to be kidnapped. If the murderers stayed true to their pattern then her early morning runs had been noted and she would be next. Beth left in her Mercedes and when she got to the park she deliberately left her purse and phone in the car, locked it and pocketed the keys.

Beth stretched and then began to jog into the park. She had expanded her senses and felt the interest from behind her. She could also feel someone ahead on the path. Foot steps behind her began to speed up. She maintained her pace pretending to be unaware of the predatory vibe she was picking up from both men. She sent a thought to Manuel, who in turn relayed it to the cats.

The men were so intent on her that they remained unaware of Will, and the cousins and Manuel who were closing in on them. The man behind Beth caught up and said, "Excuse me but I really like your shoes. Where did you get them?"

"Sheel's. Do you really like them?"

"Yes, I do."

"Did you get them at the Sheel's in Durango or where?"

"Denver on Colfax Drive. If you want to get some too they are Sketcher's."

The other hunter approached from the opposite direction and stopped in the middle of the trail where he pretended to tie his shoelace. When Beth drew even with him he grabbed her and the other hunter put a cloth smelling of chloroform over Beth's nose and mouth. She pretended to fight for a few seconds and then allowed her body to go limp. She closed her eyes and when they removed the cloth she pretended to breathe like someone asleep.

The taller of the two hoisted her onto his shoulders and proceeded to carry her to a Ryder van. He dropped her into the body of the van and shut the doors. A few moments later the van began to move and bounced over the uneven ground.

The van pulled onto a gravel road and crossed a cattle guard. A few minutes later it pulled up in front of a barn. A woman in a wheelchair was on the veranda and asked her captor where they had gone.

"Just for a ride into town and home mam." He said. "I'll be with you in just a minute."

"Well make it soon. I am hungry."

"Yes mam I brought dinner."

By this time Manuel and the cats were with in striking distance. The cats slipped silently closer to the porch. They were ready to pounce when the woman said, "What did you bring me? Did you catch another were animal? You know I should be able to transform soon and be out of this wheelchair. If their bite can make a were then eating them should work too. I wonder what we are doing wrong."

"Maybe they need to be in were form when you eat and maybe they need to be alive when you do."

"Maybe we can try it with this one."

"Yes mam. I'll fetch her for you now."

While this conversation was happening, the cats and Zack circled closer to see if the woman could leave the chair at all. Some people could briefly. They waited for the signal from Manuel to attack. Manuel held up his hand, his fist closed indicating the others wait where they were. They froze in place in the shadows next to the veranda. Their hearts and breathing were steady as they waited.

Manuel stepped put of the shadows and said, "Excuse me. My car broke down and I wonder if I could use your phone?"

The woman hissed in surprise at his sudden appearance. "How long have you been standing there?" she said, her hand reaching under the lap robe to grasp the weapon she had hidden there.

"Oh not long. You could have heard me approach but you were talking about your dinner." He chuckled. "Perhaps you should be more aware of who and what may be around you. Is there anyone else here?"

"Yes, maybe they are in the house."

"Mam, you want me to take care of this man for you?" The man had left the back door of the van and was moving slowly toward Manuel. The woman pulled her hand out from the blanket and pointed the gun at Manuel. Manuel was on her in an instant. As the gun tore from her hand, when Manuel grasped and pulled, it went off, the bullet lodged in the decking of the porch. The man tried to run to aid the woman when the back door of the van crashed open and Beth charged him from behind. In moments the humans were both incapacitated and the weres transformed to human form to search for any other people. In short order they were back with word there were no others.

"What are you?"The woman demanded an answer. "You're no were."

Beth kept silent and Manuel answered mildly, "We are vampires."

The man snorted, "Bullshit, there aren't any vampires in Colorado."

Manuel turned to the woman and stared deeply into her eyes. In a gentle voice he said, "You want to tell me who you are and why you are hunting weres and other supernaturals."

"I am Beatrice Kinder and I want to walk again I don't care if it is on four feet I just want to do it. They told me that if I ate were meat that I could walk again as a were."

"Who told you that?" Beth asked. Beatrice shook her head so Manuel asked her the same question.

"They said they belonged to the Van Helsing Society and that I could help them rid the world of dangerous animals who hurt people and I could walk if I did what they said."

"Ask her why she tortured them." Will suggested.

"Why did you torture them?"

"They wouldn't change for me and they wouldn't bite me. Besides it's not like I was hurting real people."

Will snarled deep in his chest. Manuel and Beth stared at him so he excused himself to go away from the temptation to attack her. He wandered over to the barn and his hackles rose he could smell the blood and fear that emanated from the structure before he was inside.

The shadowed interior mercifully hid much and then he heard the whimper. He pulled out his phone and used the flashlight app to see what caused the sound. What he saw made him sick to his stomach. A young were wolf cub was stretched out on an 'X' shaped frame and held suspended by nails driven into his wrists and feet. Blood trickled from lash marks that crisscrossed his slender chest. He looked to be around ten, too young to have made his first change. It was obvious that he had been there for several days. His legs were stained with urine and feces and flies were everywhere. Will spoke to him then. "Easy boy. I am going to get help and we will get you out of here." He ran from the barn calling for two of the others to come help him. They were equally horrified when they saw what had been done and Zack experienced a depth of rage he didn't know he could feel. He wanted to rend the creatures who had done such wanton acts of cruelty. He held on to his human form by the barest margin of control as he held the boy upright while the others pulled the nails from his swollen flesh. They laid the boy down then and Will went into the house and got towels and fresh water, some for him to drink and some to wash his wounds. There were no first aid supplies anywhere that he could find.

Gently they loaded the child into the back of the van where they made a soft nest of blankets and quilts. They would take him to the Doctor or rather they would have the doc come to the ranch. The wolves would take care of him once he could walk but until then it was best if he remain hidden. Zack arrested the two and then thought better of it. The vampires killed them quickly and set fire to the house and barn making sure the fire did not spread. Manuel had gotten all the information from them that they had and he discussed it with the others as they rode home to the ranch in the van.

"The Van Helsing Society is an international organization that seeks out all members of the secret world for murder. They have it as their mission to "Protect humans from the monsters" namely us. They also have no problem causing us gross physical pain because they believe that since we are not human we must be evil monsters. It doesn't matter that we were human at one point or that we contribute to society. Whatever good we achieve they claim is a slap in the face for humans. They fear us and therefore they condemn us out of hand. They say we steal work away from humans. "

"It is us and them to extremes and like any hate mongers they operate out of ignorance anger and resentment. I believe there is some jealousy mixed in as well. Chris could give you a better definition or explanation sociologically and psychologically speaking as they are her main area of interest and expertise." Will said.

Richard agreed with him. "I know my mother-in-law will be able to explain the psychology behind the hate mongering."

"You noticed they knew exactly what to use to trigger those people we just disposed of. I think it would be wise to call an emergency meeting of the council and before we meet I think we should find out what the council in the old world knows about them."

"Good. Make it a motion and those of us present can vote on it. That way we have at least three or four of the secret world to make a quorum."

"Well not really a quorum but at least a representative group." They laughed then and it lightened the atmosphere.

The boy was sleeping when they pulled up in front of the house. Chris met them and hurriedly led them to a spare bedroom which was always ready for guests. She had Jen call the doctor and while they waited for her they used their first aid kit to clean and treat the lash marks which didn't require stitches.

The boy kept drifting into and out of consciousness. Chris and Jen were worried that he wouldn't survive. He had lost a lot of blood and was seriously dehydrated. When he was conscious Jen had him suck on ice. She didn't want him to drink too much and end up puking. An hour later the doctor showed up and immediately went to work on his feet and wrists. The size of the puncture wounds made them easier to treat than anyone had realized. However they required stitching and lots of antibiotic creams and tablets. She gave him an injection which put him to sleep. Next she sutured those gashes from the whipping that had been deep enough to show bone. Finally after an hour of intensive work she had done everything possible to help the boy she contacted the George and had him check his contacts for missing children. Since the boy was of wolf kin they figured George would have a vested interest in finding his parents if they were still alive.

Meanwhile the boy would stay with the cats where he would have round the clock nursing and a doctor on call just down the hall. Only one of the cats had gone to medical school to be a general practitioner. She had retired the year before. The others were either EMTs or RNs and one of the younger cats was in residency at the Mayo Clinic in Minneapolis to be an orthopedic surgeon. George was grateful for the care they were giving the boy and said if ever they needed a favor he would be there.

CHAPTER 27

Beth, Manuel and Will called for an emergency meeting of the ISPS council to meet in Kansas City at the Ramada. They booked The large conference room and paid the hotel for three days. The idea was to appraise the rest of the new world weres as to the existence of the Van Helsing Society and their mission to rid the world of the supernaturals.

The dryads decided that the clear cutting of forests was the work of the society in an effort to rid the world of them, the elves and fairies. They determined to fight back through legal means and sabotage if that didn't work. Since the elves and fairies owned the land they lived on and the trees there they were no longer in danger of being eradicated neither were the dryads who had been transplanted a few years before. Still the wolves and other weres were concerned.

They used the forests as hunting grounds and with clear cutting the natural habitat of their traditional prey was being seriously depleted. They decided to fight in court for protection of their hunting grounds. But this was old news and the main reason for the meeting was the emergence of the Van Helsing Society and the threat they posed. First Will asked if any of the other weres and fey had any inkling of their existence. If so rather than go for the obvious question as to why they didn't tell the others he decided that it would be a waste of time and would cause dissent which they couldn't afford.

Instead he asked what they had heard and whether it was presented to them as rumor or fact. The goblins said that they had heard whispers but nothing concrete. The dwarf representatives said the same. Suggestions but no actual facts had been presented so they didn't pass it on. Will said, "I can understand that. Why jump at shadows when there are more immediate threats like poachers and hunters and the encroachment of housing developments into their habitat. The dwarves had miners to deal with too. They had begun to utilize the abandoned tunnels under the cities, like old New York subway tunnels, to get from one area to another. The elves and other fey needed sunlight and fresh air to function and so the tunnels were not an option for them. This was discussed as well.

It was decided that Will and Manuel would represent the New World ISPS and with their wives would go to visit the Old World ISPS in Munich to learn all they could about the society. This was unanimous and so they applied for passports. Six weeks later the passports were ready and Manuel called for his jet to take them to Munich. Then he let Will know that they would be using the jet. Beth was happy to be going back to Europe and wanted to spend some time in Paris shopping. Her enthusiasm spilled over on to Chris.

They announced their imminent arrival to the Council and asked to meet with them as soon as they had landed. This request was greeted with shock and grudging acquiescence. The Old World Council was not used to having demands made on them. They were the ones who made such requests of others. Still they did agree and the full council was ready to meet Will and Manuel when they landed in the evening. Chris and Beth checked in to the Hotel Athénée and were escorted to their rooms. The rooms were spacious with white walls and bedding and gold draperies and accents. The sitting area was upholstered in mauve velvet and the bathrooms were white and marble. The towels were luxuriously thick and Chris was delighted with the room. Once settled in they met in the interior courtyard where there was outside dining under red canvas umbrellas for coffee and pastry.

Chris was suitably impressed by the accommodations and Beth was delighted that her favorite hotel met Chris' enthusiasm. They wandered toward the Arc d' Triomphe and Chris soaked in the ambiance of the city. She decided that Paris was her favorite city which tickled Beth. She said "You haven't come to see us in New Orleans yet. I think you may change your mind."

"Oh but Paris is all I dreamed it would be." Chris said with absolute conviction in her voice. "I can't imagine anywhere else feeling this wonderful. The history alone makes it special."

"I have to admit that it is full of history." Beth laughed. "Do you want to go to the Arc or maybe just walk along the Champs for a little way? The men will be joining us fairly soon."

"Oh lets just sit a bit and go for a walk when they can join us."

"OK that suits me. How do you know the men will be here so soon?"

"Manuel and I have a special connection and I can feel what he is feeling." She didn't think Chris needed to know they had a telepathic link.

"Oh then lets wait for them in the dining room but lets get dressed for dinner first."

"Its a good thing you told me to bring dresses suitable for cocktails and dinner otherwise I would be wearing slacks or even jeans."

"Well I kind of knew what to expect since I have been here before and I was seriously under dressed our first night. Fortunately Manuel's family is well known and they are always catered to so no one said anything but I was embarrassed. Thank goodness I was wearing some diamonds so I wasn't as under-dressed as I would have been without them. "She laughed then. "I'll see you in the dining room after the men come here to change. In about an hour then. They are just outside now."

"Yes and I need to change too since these jeans will hardly do."Chris hurried to her room and quickly put on Will's favorite blue cocktail dress with the unique neckline and single shoulder. She put on the sapphire earrings that he bought her in Denver and with her diamond tennis bracelet and rings she looked every bit the lady she could be. She sat in the sitting area of the room after she laid out Will's tux with the black cummerbund and tie. It wasn't long before Will came in and kissed her. "You look good enough to eat." He joked.

"So will you when you get dressed. And in case you are wondering I am starving." She looked at Will with obvious lust and he said, "If you keep looking at me like that we will never make it to the dining room."

Chris laughed at him and said, "Please hurry. I really am hungry and I want to show you off. You look amazing in that suit."

Will fastened the French Cuffs of his dinner shirt with the onyx cuff links. He grabbed the jacket and as he put it on he said. "Shall we go show off our party manners?"

"I'm ready."

"Lets go show Manuel and Beth that us countrified folk can fit in in the big city too." He held out his arm and Chris took it as they left the room for the dining room and their first meal with Beth and Manuel in a formal setting.

Chris had decided to order Escargot and baked French Onion Soup to start their meal and then she ordered lamb and grilled vegetables for her main course. They enjoyed the dinner and Chris loved the variety of wines that Will ordered to go with everything. She also noticed that Manuel appeared to be impressed with his choices. That was born out when he commented on Will's choice of brandy with their coffee and on his choice of dessert wine to have with the bomb Manuel ordered for them all. "You have an excellent taste in wines my friend. Where did you learn?"

"I learned when I worked at Purgatory Ski Resort in the kitchen. The wine steward taught me. He was actually a classically trained sommelier from New York and I was curious enough to ask him about them."

"Is he the one who had a crush on you?"

"Yeah, he was very gay and was so disappointed that I wasn't. But he proved a good friend after all. I never did find out why he came to Purgatory but I was glad he did. I could talk to him about anything and not be judged."

"Real friends like that are hard to find. You are fortunate. Do you keep in touch with him?"

"Yes I hear from him once a month when we call each other and catch up on our lives. The last time I spoke to him he had fallen in love with the new sous chef at the restaurant who seemed to return his affections. The last I heard they were talking about getting married. I wished him happy." Dinner concluded and jet lag setting in the couples said good night and went to their respective rooms.

CHAPTER 28

There were several meetings with the Old World ISPS and Manuel and Will learned all the European members knew about the van Helsings. It was surprisingly little. They had come into existence following the publication of Bram

Stoker's Dracula novel. The society appeared to be made up of people who believed all sorts of bizarre things and had not been taken seriously by the ISPS. When they learned about the operations in the States they immediately went on high watch. The ISPS decided that not only would the high alert remain in place indefinitely the ISPS would actively hunt the members of the van Helsing organization for interrogation and disposal. It was to be war. The like of which had never been seen before. The elves and other Fey would use their members as advance spotters and then the weres and vampires would take care of the rest. They would team one vampire to each were group. It made sense since the weres could intimidate and the vampires could force confessions just as Manuel had done with the woman in Colorado.

This was one of the least debated sessions the council had ever had and they were proud of their speedy decision making. The elders congratulated Will and Manuel on their ability to work together and they hoped for the same degree of cooperation from those in the old world. They ended the session quickly. Since Will and Manuel had told the council at home that they would be gone a week they decided to use the extra time as tourists. They went to the Louvre and to Versailles. They had dinner on a boat on the Seine and went to a wine tasting. They explored the Left Bank and had coffee in the cafe where Toulouse La Trek did some of his sketches of can-can dancers. All in all they had a wonderful week. The girls went shopping and Beth introduced Chris to her favorite designers.

At the end of the week they boarded the jet for home with more packages than they had arrived with and their staff laughingly put everything away for Beth. They had dinner on board as they chased the sun across the Atlantic and they played Canasta during the final leg of the journey. Their pilot dimmed the lights when Night caught them approaching New York and their refueling stop. Everyone was asleep as the plane took off for Colorado.

CHAPTER 29

Home again, Chris and Will said good bye to Manuel and Beth. They would be notifying the rest of the supernatural community with what they had learned about the Van Helsing Society. Manuel would be going to Central and South America in a week to let them know about the society so they could be on their guard. He planned to set up a more regular line of communication with them.

While Will was gone. Richard, Chris and Jen took control of the weres and set up new rules for them. One rule never to be broken was being away from home alone. There would be no more solitary walks. If any of the community needed to go somewhere they had to find a partner to travel with. This was especially hard on the weres as they tended to take solitary jaunts into the mountains. Now that the dryads were all back east there was no early warning system for such journeys, With the van Helsings about to do so would be foolhardy to say the least. Chris insisted that the young be kept close to home. No more games of hide and seek in the woods. If they were sent to gather items from the garden they were to be accompanied by an adult. If no adult was available then they did not go.

Another new rule was that no one went out at night unless they went in a group of four or more. This included trips to the Fox and Hound where the main subject under discussion was the Van Helsings.

Chris also insisted that the community went armed. She made a schedule so that everyone had marksmanship practice on a weekly basis. She and the others agreed that the ability to protect each other was of paramount importance. Strangers were looked on with suspicion if they were traveling alone or as a same sex couple. It made sense to all the community members that they follow Chris' guide lines for keeping them safe. Although it must be admitted that the teens found them to be stultifying in the extreme. They were very vocal in their resentment and believed that if they did things as a group they should not require an armed adult to protect them.

Chris made it clear that they might think they were prepared to take care of themselves but they had no defense against chloroform. "All it takes is a few seconds of breathing the fumes and you would be unconscious and unable to change. Therefore you will do as instructed or pay the price with your life." The teens backed down when they saw what had been done to their aunt. Chris had no compunctions about showing them the crime scene photos. As a result three very chagrined teens apologized and promised to abide by the new rules. Chris and Will had doubts about how long they would remember but decided that they would wait and see as Lavender was especially head strong and had a serious devil may care attitude about most things.

CHAPTER 30

One of their friends, a were wolf child, was having a birthday party. It was a sweet sixteen party and the first one she could have with boys too. The girls were as excited about going as the wolf was in having the party. Jen wasn't sure it was a good idea but it was summer. They planned on going to the lake and the wolves were sure that there was safety in numbers. The girl's parents planned to be there as chaperons. They would also tend the bonfire. They would be armed in case their plans were discovered by the van Helsings.

The girls met with their friend at the coffee shop and in usual headlong fashion discussed the location for the party and who all would be there. They had no regard for who else was there. Being teens meant being louder than adults or children. There were strangers, tourists, in the coffee shop who couldn't help overhearing the excited plans.

Saturday came and with it the time for the party. The wolves picked up the twins and Jen's final words to them were, "Remember to stay with the group and have fun. I love you."

"Aw, mom. We'll be good." Lavender said and they were gone. Jen thought about going in cat form to help with security but Will and Chris talked her out of it. That was a mistake.

Jasmine and Lavender packed backpacks with towels, swimsuits, and sweaters for when the night got cooler. Hair brushes and makeup added they were ready to go. Chris and Jen hugged them and told them to have fun. Jasmine smiled shyly and said, "Yes mam. OK mom."

The party was in full swing when couples tried to slip away for some making out sessions and Jen and Richard and Will and Chris were hard pressed to keep track. There were over a hundred kids present for the party. Many of whom had heard about it from a friend and just showed up. Patty, the wolf's child whose party it was, was thrilled at the attendance. She had no idea she was so popular. The couples were eventually missed and a search was conducted. Many were found in compromising positions but the adults were not taking them to task for that. What they were in trouble for was leaving the group for the isolation of the woods. George stopped by and brought two of his deputies with him to help with crowd control. Around midnight the bonfire was almost gone and many of the party goers had left for home when one of the humans who had come to the party came to the sheriff. Her date was missing. He was a wolf from the next county. She had been looking for him for the past hour and was becoming angry at him for ditching her. She had heard about the party and had invited him. George got his name and description from the girl. His deputies would begin a search of the woods near the party area and then spread outward. They had his scent from the sweater he had left in the girl's car. Under the guise of close examination the deputies and George got the scent.

It wasn't long before George picked up his trail and with it was the sickening smell of chloroform. It was obvious from the urine that the boy had gone into the woods to relieve himself. George notified Richard and Will right away. The van Helsings had learned of the party and struck.

There was an odor of fear mixed into the scent and George couldn't tell if it was from the van Helsing members or from the wolf's child, one Dennis Morgan. Dennis was the only offspring of a family of surgeons who practiced medicine in both counties. They were well liked and respected through out the were community and by humans. Dennis was also on the high school varsity football team and a member of the honor society. He also played bassoon in the orchestra. Very popular well liked kid and George and the others were desperate to find him before much more time passed. They left the girl with Jen and along with Chris followed the trail to a small cabin.

Light from an oil lamp made a welcoming glow from the windows of the one room structure. The fallen needles from the yellow pine and juniper acted to quiet their approach. George knocked on the door just as an eerie howl sounded from within. The boy had awakened and sensing danger had transformed. The humans had him cornered next to the wood burning stove and one wall of the cabin. He was snarling and snapping at the humans who were trying to capture him. George and Will saw all this as they broke down the door.

George fired his pistol into the air to get everyone's attention. Shocked silence greeted his action and the humans tried to bluff. "How dare you interfere with us? We are on a mission from God and you interrupt at your peril." This was said by a human who looked to be in his thirties and was obviously the leader of the three. He stood tall at about six foot two with blonde hair and blue eyes. A scar bisected his left cheek that looked to have been caused by a claw.

"You are in violation of state laws regarding the ownership of exotic pets. I am here to write you a ticket. You will receive a court date by mail. If you fail to appear a bench warrant will be issued for your arrest and your name and description with a photo will be circulated among the police departments across the country. Do I make myself clear?" George announced.

"We don't own this wolf!"One of the younger people blurted out.

The older of the humans hissed with displeasure. "Be quiet."

"Sorry sir, I was trying to help."

"I said to be quiet."

The thirty year old moved in front of the wolf cub and made a fatal error; he turned his back. The wolf jumped on him knocking him to the floor of the cabin. The cattle prod the man had been holding fell away as the cub broke his neck with one powerful shake of his head. The two youths who had accompanied the older man froze in shock. "Oh my God!" Shouted the one who had spoken before. "Oh my God! It killed him." He turned to run and was met by two snarling mountain lions. Will and Richard had transformed while attention had been centered on the play between George and the human. They made quick work of killing the other two van Helsing members.

Meanwhile George had calmed Dennis and he transferred back to human. "That bastard hit me with the cattle prod so I transformed." His voice shook with suppressed anger. His silver eyes were partially hidden by narrowed lids. "Did I kill him?"

"Yes, he's dead."

"I've never killed a human before. I..." His voice broke. "I..."

"Its tough the first time, lad. You were raised to respect human life. I know your family." George sighed, "They will understand if you choose to tell them and they can help you deal with it if you let them."

Dennis raised his head. Tears glistened on his cheeks. "Yes, sir. I'll have to talk to them about it. My dad will understand I think."

"Time to leave and to get you home."

CHAPTER 31

George and the others took Dennis back to the party area and found nearly everyone gone.

Dennis murmured something to low for human ears to catch but all the weres heard him say. "I'm fine Lidia, some bad men kidnapped me when I went into the trees to use the bathroom but George, Richard and Will rescued me. I'm fine just upset by it all." He kissed her then and she snuggled under his arm.

"As long as you are alright." She whispered. "I was so mad at you! I'm so sorry."

She placed her arm around his waist and held him tight.

Will and Richard looked at each other and grinned. George winked at them over the boy's head. "I think he'll be just fine." He said to the air in general. The girl, Lidia, looked surprised for a moment because she hadn't realized she had spoken aloud. Then she smiled and the girl who had merely appeared pleasing to the eye became radiant. George nodded solemnly. He could see the attraction she held for Dennis. "Well do you want me to go explain to your mother and father why you are out past your curfew? I will be happy to explain it to them Lidia."

"Oh yes, please. I am sure they are worried which means they are getting angry."

"Well come along then. Let's get you home." Then to Dennis he said, "Are you ready to go home too?" At Dennis' nod he said, "I am going to send Will with you and he will corroborate your statements when you tell your parents what happened. I want him to explain about the Van Helsing Society to them as well. One of the deputies will follow along to drive him back home when you are done."

"Thank you Sheriff Mac Govern. I appreciate it." He bent down and kissed Lidia softly. "I'll call you later. OK?"

"Oh yes." Lidia answered a bit breathlessly.

George took Lidia's arm as he led her toward the squad car. He ushered her into the front and settled in to drive her home. "You'll have to give me directions." Lidia agreed and began.

Twenty minutes later they pulled up in front of a modest ranch style house with a well tended lawn and an apple tree in the front yard. The flower beds along the front walk were freshly mulched. George nodded approvingly. Every light in the house was on and George could see the shadow of someone pacing the front room.

Lidia opened the door and she and George went in. Fortunately George was in uniform because it took a moment for his presence to register with the highly irate father. "Sheriff Mac Govern. I'm Lidia's father. What has she done? Why are you bringing her home and not her date?"

"She is late because we had trouble at the lake. Some real lowlifes kidnapped one of the guests, Dennis Richard Morgan, your daughter's date. We were able to recover him but that all took time and it is why she is late. She is safe and sound and the miscreants have been dealt with. She was in no danger. I must say she has great presence of mind and handled the situation better than some adults would. You have a girl to be proud of sir. She is the one who alerted us to the trouble and it is thanks to her quick thinking that the boy was recovered before he was hurt. They had chloroformed him."

Lidia's mother hurried forward and enfolded her daughter in a hug. "Thank god you are alright and they weren't after you too."

"I wasn't in any danger. They took Denny when he went into the woods to use the bathroom. I think they knew who he was. They knew he was the reason we were going to the regionals for football. I think they kidnapped him to keep our team from winning."

"Is that right?"

"Oh yes, they confessed."George agreed and reminded himself that that was the story the media would have. He admired Lidia's quick thinking and realized that the mention of the football team had completely mollified her father. "If you are all alright I need to get busy on the paperwork surrounding this case. I think you have a wonderful daughter. She is quick thinking and responsible for us catching the bad guys. Now I really must go. I wish you all goodnight. I'll see myself out." What could have resulted in unpleasantness, ended with parents telling their daughter how proud of her they were. George grinned a wolfish smile as he drove away from the house. She would make a wonderful addition to the wolves if he read Dennis right.

CHAPTER 32

Jen and Chris waited impatiently for their men to return to pick them up from the party site. While they waited they collected paper cups and plates and put them into the dwindling flames of the bonfire. They believed in leaving a campsite

131

cleaner than they found it. Soda and beer cans were set aside and so was the food that was left over. There wasn't much of the latter. The cans would go to be recycled.

By the time Will and Richard returned the campsite was pristine and the women were starting to be concerned. "Hi. What took you so long?" Jen queried. "I thought you were just taking the kids home."

"Hi yourself. We did but Dennis' parents needed an explanation. We told them about the kidnap attempt and about the Van Helsing Society in more detail than the general announcement had given. They had some questions and of course we had to answer them. Then too they were questioning their son about his role in his rescue. He broke down as he described his attack on the kidnapper. With tear stained face he looked hopefully at his mother and father. He desperately wanted them to tell him it would be alright. That he had no choice. His mother hugged him and his father asked to see the burn site from the cattle prod. Dennis raised his shirt so his dad could examine the oddly shaped marks of the prongs. The marks dragged for an inch or more across the boy's belly.

Dennis explained about how frightened he was when he woke up to be hit with the cattle prod. He had howled with the pain. That was when George, Will and Richard had come in with a deputy and everything that followed. He spoke about his attack on the kidnapper and that he had killed him. He shook with reaction. His mother held him tighter and his father said. "It seems to me that you had no choice. You ruined an enemy's hopes and protected yourself the only way possible given the circumstances. You will have bad dreams for a while while your brain reconciles what happened with what you have been taught. But we are here for you and we will see that you get counseling help if you need it. You did well given what happened to you."

"Thank you father. I'm exhausted."

"So you should be, given what has happened to you. Your mother will see you upstairs and I will come after I speak with Will." Will and Richard waited for them to leave and to address the Hippo in the room.

"Your son was provoked past all reasoning and showed remarkable restraint when he jumped on his attacker. He could have torn him apart but he chose to break the man's neck instead. We are proud of this wolf. Stop by the office and I will give him his medal for heroic citizenship."

"Sir I don't need a medal." Dennis stopped by the door and said it again. "I don't need it."

"Maybe not but your children will be very proud of your accomplishment in caring for the welfare of all fey. According to the rules regulating the presentation, your actions were exactly what the medal was designed to promote. I would like to have some media coverage of the presentation but given that it was for action as a were, that will not happen. However Henry and the deputy will spread word in the were community though. Now you need to get to bed."

"Yes sir."

"Come along now Denny." His mother urged him.

"OK mom." He headed for the stairs and his bedroom. His mother followed.

"I want to know how such a thing could happen and whether my son was the intended target or they just chose him by opportunity."

"As to how it could happen the kids were discussing the party in a public place and were overheard. Your son was simply in the wrong place at the wrong time. As he told you he went into the trees to go to the bathroom and that is where they grabbed him. They chloroformed him and took him to that old miner's cabin about a mile away from the lake. They had barely started to torture him when we showed up and interrupted them. They must have wanted him in wolf form because he was not restrained the way other victims were. The funny thing is is that they could as easily have caught a human as there were quite a few at the party. We don't know yet why they wanted a were and one to change. I think they may want to be able to change as well but as I said, I don't know."

"It seems to me that you really don't know very much at all. Why didn't you question them?"

"We felt it was more important to get your son home."Richard said.

"The ISPS has set the guide lines for handling the Van Helsings and I think they are wrong. I think rather than killing each member we come across we should take the time to question them. I intend to call an emergency meeting of the council as soon as possible to discuss it."

"Well I should think you would have done so already." He bristled. "You are supposed to be in charge after all."

"We were unaware of how serious the problem was. We based our actions on the recommendations of the Old World ISPS." He snapped. "I wont make that mistake again. Now we need to leave and work with the sheriff to find out if they were the only enemy in the area. We will keep in touch as you need to know given Dennis' involvement." Richard said mildly.

Dennis' mother came in then and said, "You can't call those animals human. They don't deserve the honor!"

"They are not supernatural therefor they classify as human. Now we really must go. We have much to do before we can sleep." Will said.

"I'll see you out." Doctor Morgan said.

"Thank you."Will replied.

"See you set that meeting soon."

"I shall be making the calls in the morning and I will include the members in Central and

South America. If the Van Helsings are here, they are there too.”

The door closed behind them and Will breathed a sigh of relief. “That went better than I thought it would.” Will and Richard got into the squad car and headed back to the lake and their wives. The party had wound down and only Chris and Jen were left when they arrived.

CHAPTER 33

When Chris and the others arrived home it was to a fully lit house and a household stirring like a hive of bees. “What’s going on?”One of the junior weres held out a telegram.

To the current head of the local chapter of the ISPS: This is to notify you that it is with deep regret we must report the passing of Marcus and Rosa in a freak snowmobile accident. They were caught by an avalanche and we were unable to reach them in time to save them. We have their remains at our local funeral home and await your instructions. Sincerely. And it was signed by the local Chief of Police one James Johnson.
Christine fell apart as did Jennifer Marie. “Oh god it is just too much.” Jen sobbed.

Richard held her, his tears dampening her hair as she cried in his arms. Will held his tears as he comforted Chris. “They went together which is the way it is with life mates. Whichever one died first the other would follow within hours. We will die that way my love. It is the way of our kind. You know that don't you?"

"Ye...ye...yes I know but that doesn't make it any easier to know they are gone." Her tears slowed and she looked at Will with desperation. "I only hope I go first. I don't think I could abide two or three hours of total despair. I would go mad."

"You are stronger than that my love."

"No I am not, but it is time to plan the memorial and the life celebration for them not for me to wallow in what may happen." She took a deep breath, "Why don't you call the other council members and especially the neighbors down south and I will contact George and Henry and give them the news." Chris blew her nose and gave Will a quick hug. "Make love to me later." She whispered. And she blew him a kiss. She turned and reached for the phone. She used the speed dial and called George first.

Phone calls made she went to the room she shared with Will and got into bed. She knew she should shower and get rid of the smoke smell from the bonfire but she didn't have the energy. Maybe just this once she could skip it. She was asleep when Will came in to cuddle her limp form against him. He was asleep within minutes.

Will had called all the representatives of the council who had worked with Marcus to tell them the sad news and to warn them about the Van Helsing Society. Then he had called the members down south of the border. In Spanish and

Portuguese he told them about the Van Helsings and the sad news of Marcus' passing. His Portuguese was very rudimentary and it was fortunate that the representative spoke English. He answered Will with a very British accent. When Will asked him where he had learned it he was informed that Seignior Gonzales had gone to boarding school in England. He offered to spread the word about Marcus to the others and Will said, "I appreciate the offer but I have already done so the only ones left are Venezuela and Peru."

"Well I will be happy to assist you in that."

"Very well. I shall tell my council members and we will send a representative for the Memorial service. Will he be buried or cremated?"

"We cremate our dead."

"Very good then let me know when you are holding the service and one of us shall be there. Via con Dios."

All the councilors that Will contacted had made the same offer to attend the memorial and he was gratified. He said that he would notify them as soon as he knew the answer as to when it would be held.

Will's dreams were a disturbing mix of attacks by Van Helsings and a well armed and powerful racial purity group. Fortunately it was only a dream. The Van Helsings did not have the backing to hire mercenaries to kill all the supernaturals. He awoke with a plan and called Manuel.

The supers had the where with all to hire the best mercenaries. However, it was decided to use the investigators who worked for Manuel and the vampires to find their home base if they had one.

CHAPTER 34

The next thing that was decided was that the Brownies and other household fey would infiltrate the homes of the Van Helsing organization, as they were discovered, and spy on them. If the supernatural world could learn their plans then those plans could be circumvented. Once the enemy was identified and their plans discerned then it would be time to remove them from the board.

It would prove to be more difficult than anticipated. The Van Helsings were set up in cells with no one member knowing the next higher up in the organization. All directives and information came from the top down through safe drops.

CHAPTER 35

Chris and Will decided to have a standard non denominational religious service although they were members of the Episcopal church. They never saw Marcus or Rosa attend a service anywhere. Marcus used to say working in his garden was his worship service so a non denominational service was ideal. Then the local Catholic priest, Father Wilson, came to Will asking why, since they were Catholic, he was not conducting the service. Will was amazed. He had no idea and said so.

"Why yes we have a rite for them and I shall be happy to conduct it as soon as possible. Now what about the service for the dead? You need someone to conduct the prayers and a choir to sing and there is the service to read."

"Yes, of course Father Wilson. We will be honored to have you conduct the service." Will thought fast. He supposed that the life celebration could go ahead as planned even though the grave side service would be Catholic and they would have the Catholic church service too. Will hoped that the change in plans wouldn't discommode Chris too much.

Henry was talking about having the Life Celebration at the Fox and Hound. He said and Will agreed, that it was large enough to hold everyone and it was the perfect venue since Marcus used to spend quite a bit of his off time there. His social skills were phenomenal and everyone loved him who got to know him. Also there was the weekly poker game Marcus had enjoyed.

Chris thought it was a wonderful idea and backed Henry completely. So it was decided. The Friday night following the funeral would be the celebration and Henry would close the Fox to outsiders. This was vital as there could be enemy about and it would be only too easy for them to identify more weres to kidnap and kill if they were allowed inside. Of course part of the celebration would be a cooperative hunt. The wolves and bears would join the cats and the hunt would take place north of Purgatory away from the ski and snow mobile trails. There they could change without worrying about being seen.

A herd of mule deer frequented a large meadow there where the Game Warden set out salt licks that the deer loved. He had made sure they could reach the grasses that grew in profusion by scraping away most of the snow with his Arctic Cat with the plow attachment. That way they could scrape away the rest with sharp hooves.

The hunt went well and they were able to cull the herd. Those deer too old to run or those who were sick fell prey to the wolves, Henry and the cats. They transformed and carried the dead animals with them to their vehicles. This would feed many for the remainder of the winter and the spring. All totaled they took five culls. They left no trace of their hunt for the ranger to worry over except for the odd footprint. They knew the deer would return and that was what mattered most.

The day following the hunt was Marcus and Rosa's funeral and cremation. "The dust to dust and ashes to ashes" was particularly appropriate when they thought about it. Will was a brick for Chris as she cried silently. He wrapped a comforting arm around her shoulders. They knelt and stood and sat at all the appropriate times during the service. They sang chants and hymns like Nearer My God to Thee and Marcus' favorite hymn, The Battle Hymn of the Republic. Rosa never stated a preference so for her the choir sang Amazing Grace. Their coffins were covered with blankets of roses and lilies. There were so many bouquets that the front of the church looked like a flower shop.

Following the service the couple were transported to the funeral home and were cremated. Their ashes were taken to their favorite places and spread in the wind. The urns were placed on the mantle in the Fox and Hound to be used again when it was appropriate.

The following Friday everyone gathered at the Fox and Hound for an open bar and stories abounded about them. Someone told their favorite jokes and everyone reminisced about Marcus and Rosa. Funny stories were told about them like the time Rosa's doctor saw her at the grocery store and when she appeared not to recognize him, spoke to her. She responded, "Oh Doc I didn't know you with your clothes on!"Everyone laughed. That was fairly typical of the stories they told.

It was an excellent wake. Members of the ISPS council who had worked with Marcus were in attendance too and had their own stories to share. Those who had either worked with or had known Rosa shared stories that spoke of her love for her extended family and what an artist she was in the kitchen.

CHAPTER 36

Chris and Will aged and soon enough were great grandparents. Lavender and Jasmine married and moved in with their husbands' families. Their cubs were born twins and were doted on by the girls and by their grand parents. The boys grew quickly and were soon playing hide and seek with their sitters. They were a handful of curiosity and trouble. In fact they were very reminiscent of their great grandmother Christine.

Meanwhile the others hunted for the members of the Van Helsing Society. They had identified cells in the US and in Europe. So far Asia and Africa did not have any that could be found and the council discovered a racial prejudice on the part of the Van Helsings. To them the idea was to purify the Caucasian race. The others didn't matter to them.

The Van Helsings believed that the other races were sub human and not worth the bother. They believed that only Caucasians were made in the image of God. Other people were put on Earth to serve them and nothing else. Of course it was nonsense and the weres were horrified by the callus disregard the Van Helsings showed for the feelings of others. Their brand of patriotism was against everything the country had been established to protect and promote. And yet they claimed that they followed a higher purpose.

They believed that the orientals were part of an organization designed to take control of the world's finances. As such they were fair game and should be hurt and killed with impunity. They also believed that those whose ancestry could be traced back to Africa were created to be servants and to do any job the white man didn't want to do like being maids or dishwashers in restaurants. In fact they believed that being trash collectors was the perfect job for them. There was a strange sort of logic to what they believed but it was based on a gross fallacy which made it nonsense. Some of the best writers, artists, and inventors were of African or oriental descent but the Van Helsings denied the possibility. According to them the artists, writers and inventors stole their accomplishments from Caucasians.

The were community and the ISPS were equally determined that such ignorance should be snuffed out before it could spread to the general public. The supernatural community was horrified by the obdurate sentiments of their self declared enemies, the Van Helsings. They had the right to express an opinion but not to act on it. Their whole conspiracy theory about the idea that the weres posed a threat to society was absurd and no one with half a brain would believe it. Of course no one would believe the weres existed either if they had any sense. Werewolves were things in horror books and movies not the real world. The weres had spent centuries disproving their existence. They had no intention of allowing the Van Helsings to prove otherwise. Therefore they worked with the rest of the supernatural world to remove the threat they posed. The idea was that if they were discovered to be real then people would begin to question whether other supposed fantasy beings might exist. It would be a time of desperation as they would be hunted down and exterminated through ignorance. Better to remain subjects for horror and romance novels. At least that was the belief of the ISPS and seemed to reflect the general consensus of opinion among the supernatural community.

Will spearheaded the efforts to fictionalize the weres through the sale of books in his store and in chain stores like B Dalton. He found that the romance novels about vampires sold well as did books about werewolves so he encouraged their sale. He also made sure that the young cubs were taught to hide their otherness from any human friends. Having human friends was not encouraged but it was not actively discouraged either. Will knew from experience that the best way to insure rebellion would be to make demands about friendships. He had seen it with his own daughter, Jennifer Marie when she was young. Fortunately he had been prevented from doing too much in that direction; Chris had kept him from making that mistake more than once. Still there were some were parents who felt that mixing with humans was a sure road to disaster and they did try to dissuade their offspring from forming close friendships with them. Their main fear was that the child would be too trusting and would tell their human friend about being other. That in order to prove it they would change form to show the friend that they were harmless. Of course that wouldn't work. The fictionalized were was always a wolf and became a ravening beast when he changed shape which was always at the full moon. That last was nonsense although the full moon did pull at them it wasn't so strong that they had to change in its light. Also not all weres were male. If that were the case they would have died out centuries ago.

Still in the fictional world they were males who were cursed by a gypsy or a witch for some offense. They killed indiscriminately and they ate from what they killed, which were usually lovely young human women. Also they could transform someone with a single bite in their wolf form. In reality it took an extended period and more than one exchange of bodily fluid like saliva or sperm. This was all information the young cubs received when they approached the age for their first transformation. That transformation happened around puberty. For boys it happened when their voice changed and for girls when they had their first period. Being teenagers had their own problems. Everything from having a date for

Friday night or Saturday night to what kind of clothes to buy to express ones individuality. Of course the whole idea of being an individual with a particular style made one part of a group of like minded people so it was wasted effort.

The twins, Jasmine and Lavender, had stretched their parents' patience to the near breaking point. Especially when they started dating and picked human boys. Jennifer had nearly torn her hair out with worry. But eventually they settled down with nice were cats from California. The girls had met the males while going to school in Berkeley. Chris and Will were always happy when they came to visit. They were very proud of their girls. They felt that all the stress and worry were worth it when they had graduated from California State University with honors. Yes, they had found their husbands on campus. Like attracted like in this case and they were able to tell their new boyfriends were were cats like themselves from their pheromones. The rest as they say was history. They fell in love and were lucky enough to find life mates, a rare occurrence.

They married in California and Jen, Richard, Will and Chris went out to witness the ceremony. The wedding was held in Santa Barbara in a beautiful park overlooking the ocean. After the ceremony the twins and their new mates took Will, Chris, Richard and Jen on a brief tour ending at the beach. They were surprised to find it a rocky expanse and not the sandy stretch they had expected. Still it was a lovely town and they enjoyed their time there.

The California weres were happy to be meeting their representative to the ISPS council and made much of him. He was wined and dined by the weres who lived in and near Santa Barbara. Chris was a little disappointed at not being able to lay on the beach to get a tan but the rocks were just too uncomfortable for all they were rounded from the waves.

Although Chris thought the pervasive smell of the eucalyptus trees was pleasant and rather bracing, she felt it masked too much. How could you smell an enemy if all that you could smell was eucalyptus? Regardless she loved the feel of the town and the friendliness of the people she met. "If you ever retire, I think we should come here." She told Will with a smile. "What do you think?"

"I think it will be a long time in the future and I thought of Washington or Oregon for the hunting."

"Oh I didn't think of that, but we can hunt in the hills here."

"True. We should check out other places too though don't you think?"

"Well yes, I suppose so." This sounded slightly doubtful but at least she was keeping an open mind.

Will thought southern Utah would be ideal. It was clearly time to take her on an extended camping trip so she could see the amazing beauty there. He bet she would change her mind. Yes, it was nearly time to find a replacement for his manager-ship of the book store. He had been finding it difficult to be a proper manager and full time representative for the ISPS since the incursion of the Van Helsing Society. He still wanted to spend all his waking time with his beloved Chris and that was impossible.

CHAPTER 37

After spending a week in California the two couples returned home to Southern Colorado. While they had been gone one of the bear cubs had gone missing and a search had been launched. He was found in an abandoned mine shaft in not too bad a shape for his experience. He was a bit bruised and very thirsty. He said he had been running from some strangers and hadn't been watching where he was going.

It was shortly after that George announced he was retiring as sheriff and that he was recommending one of his deputies as a replacement. She was sharp and good at spotting little details in crime scenes and from witness testimony. George called her his female Sherlock Holmes. Will heartily approved. When a new cinnamon colored bear showed up in her territory she quickly determined that this was not a bi-natured bear and so left her alone. This proved to be a mistake as she was killed by hunters and her skin removed for taxidermy. The new sheriff was horribly upset since there was no season for bears, She determined to hunt down and prosecute the perpetrators.

Her hunt started at the sight where they had skinned the bear, and there she picked up a mixture of odors. Much of the scent had dissipated but she was able to get a strong whiff of Ralph Lauren and the odor of single malt scotch. She traced the smell to a logging road and the smell of the exhaust from the vehicle. It had a unique signature as it was burning oil as well as gas. She and the wolves and bears traced the vehicle to a farm on the east side of Durango. Although she wanted to tear them apart she fined them each five thousand dollars for poaching and she confiscated their rifles. She left them their shotgun and pistols as she had no reason to seize them as well. She also warned them about hunting from the road, including logging trails.

All in all she was proud of the way she handled the situation. George thought she did an excellent job and told her so then he reminded her about the Van Helsings and their vendetta. "Don't forget to examine the papers of strangers who hang about with no apparent reason."

"Don't worry George I will."

George nodded and gave her the keys to his squad car. "It is all yours." He announced. He and his wife took their long anticipated vacation. They had been meaning to take one for years but there

150

never seemed to be an appropriate time. Something that required the sheriff's attention always seemed to come up.

It was August when they left and on their journey they discovered berry patches. George's wife Helen had bought the accouterments for making jelly and jam. When they reached Oregon they started collecting Black Berries and they gathered enough to make a dozen jars of jam and a dozen jars of jelly. Once in the mountains they were able to find Currants and that accounted for another dozen jars. Helen would be giving a jar of each to their friends for Christmas. The exception was Henry who as a bear adored berries of all sorts so Helen made sure she had enough jelly and jam made to give him two of each.

Their trip not only took them to the Pacific Northwest but also through South Dakota, North Dakota, Wyoming and Montana where they got the currants. In Idaho they went to an opal mine where they found some nice size opals suitable for earrings.

In Oregon they had Pacific Geoduck Clams for the first time and Helen said it was a good thing that she hadn't seen them before they tried eating it because it looked like a wrinkled penis. She said, "There is no way I would have tried it if I had seen it first." She chuckled wickedly. "There are certain things you just don't eat cooked only raw."

George looked at her in amazement when she said that. She had always seemed to him to be rather demure and ladylike so such a blatant sexual reference was totally unexpected. He was quite shocked and said so. "You surprised me." He said "I never would have thought you would say anything like that in a million years."

Helen laughed gaily and said, "Oh my dear, you have much to learn about women in general and me in particular. Gentlemen are not the only ones who make sexual innuendos in mixed company. We are usually just less obvious than men." She laughed harder at his outraged expression. Chris smothered a laugh at that.

"Well I have not had them because they were out of season when we were there. What are they like? Are they chewy like calamari? How do they taste?" Chris asked.

"No, they are very sweet like sea bass and have a texture like scallops. You would love it."

"They sound yummy." Chris said licking her lips in anticipation. "So we need to go in August love." This was to Will.

"I think so." He replied with an indulgent smile. "I definitely think so."

Conversation became more general after that and Will told George about the general doings at the ranch and in town. Chris supplied details when he left something out.

There wasn't much he didn't cover and he told then about the bear hunters and how well the new sheriff had handled the situation. George told him that he had already known from having contact with her throughout their vacation. Helen said, "Oh yes they spoke every Sunday night." She sounded irritated and Chris could understand completely. She knew how she would feel if Will did something similar when he retired as chair of the local ISPS. She sincerely glad that when Will finally did retire from chairing the ISPS he would trust Richard enough to let him run things his own way. Richard was doing a great job with the bookstore and as far as she could tell Will was giving him his head as manager.

Later that night when they had gone to bed alone after they made tender love, Chris asked Will when he planned to turn the reins of the ISPS over to Richard. "I had thought to do it after New Years and announce the change to the others the same way Marcus had done with me. Will you mind?"

"Not even a little." Chris snuggled into Will's side. "I'll have you all to myself."

CHAPTER 38

It was early evening when Henry transformed and was taking a walk to clear his head. He had thought to turn the Fox and Hound over to Jim Baransky a were bear who had moved into the area a few years before and who he had hired as a bar tender. Jim had proved his worth and for the past year had been acting as assistant manager, running inventory and hiring and firing help. Henry shook his head. Yes, it was time to retire.

He was getting slow and had actually served a minor last night. It didn't matter that she had a fake ID. Anyone could see it was fake but he hadn't caught it. Yes, he was getting too old to be running a place with clientele as diverse as The Fox. He didn't need to have a reputation for serving under age kids. Fortunately she had been caught out by one of the waitresses and made to leave. Still Henry thought he should have seen the fakery. He would be a damn fool if he didn't turn the Fox over. Henry was a bear of a man at six foot four inches and he weighed about three hundred pounds of solid muscle. His hair was a rich burnt sienna as were his eyes. Everyone who knew him loved him. He was always ready with a joke or pointed comment and he was a great raconteur. His stories were always in demand.

He turned around and headed toward home. He never saw the hunter until it was too late and he was hit by a slug that caught him in the shoulder. The shock of the bullet hitting made him stumble and he rolled down the steep incline landing in the stream below. He got to his feet and moved rapidly down stream. Around a curve he climbed the bank and hissed with pain. The bullet was still in his shoulder and his arm felt heavy, as though he couldn't lift it. The hunter had lost sight of him and so he transformed to human and ran for his chalet. He made it without leaving much for the hunter to follow and called the sheriff's office. One of the wolves answered the phone and Henry told him about the hunter and that he had been shot.

He must have passed out then because the next thing he knew was that Doc Morgan was there and had just pulled the bullet from his shoulder. He groaned.

"Welcome back Henry. I want you to rest for the next few days. No exertion and stay away from work for at least the next two or three days. Definitely no heavy lifting. You let your employees do any stocking. Do you understand? Let young Jim take over for a bit."

"Yes Doc. I will."

"You are getting too old for these shenanigans." Doc Morgan frowned. "So mind you do. Well you are all patched up and I'll want to see you in my office tomorrow to change the dressing."

"Yes Doc."

"I left some pain killers for you to take. Trust me, you'll need them once the shot I gave you wears off. Now I..."His pager interrupted what he had been about to say." He checked the number and said, "I'll see you tomorrow." With that he was gone and Henry breathed a sigh of relief. The last thing he needed was a lecture on responsibility and his age. He reached for his phone and speed dialed Jim's number. Time to let go of the reins at least temporarily.

Meanwhile the sheriff and her deputies had left to follow Henry's back trail. They wanted to catch the poacher in the worst way. Henry was a favorite with the wolves. They spent part of their off time at The Fox and Hound and he let them sleep in the back room if they got too drunk to drive. He monitored their consumption and would cut them off if he thought they had enough alcohol unless they were dealing with something traumatic.

Henry had no idea the regard they held for him. To him they were good kids who deserved to decompress at his establishment. Their job was extremely stressful and being bi-natured just made it that much more so. He even had a special room set aside for them in the back next to the beer cooler. It had served as a gathering place for law enforcement personnel since he had bought The Fox and Hound fifty years before.

Jim answered on the fifth ring. He sounded groggy and Henry realized that it was six o'clock in the morning and a time when bar personnel were all sleeping. "Jim, it's Henry. I need you to manage the bar for the next few days. I've been injured and need to rest according to the doctor. You'll have to open and close if it wont be too much of a problem."

"Um, No problem Henry. What happened? Did you have a fall or what?"

"No, I was shot by a poacher and..."

"Man, you are lucky to be alive." Jim sounded wide awake. "Of course I'll do it for you. You can count on me. What do you want me to do with the receipts and the evening's take?"

"Can you run it to the bank after you close in the morning?"

"Sure or I can just put it in the safe for when you get back."

"That wont work because you will need to buy change."

"Oh right, I forgot about that. So the bank in the morning it is. You just take it easy and leave everything to me."

Henry could hear the sleepy murmur of a feminine voice in the background. "Sorry I disturbed you so early. I'm glad I didn't interrupt anything?"

Jim laughed, "No sir, boss. Not this late."

Henry laughed, "Take care Jim. And call me if you need anything, anything at all."

"OK. Bye boss."

"Bye, Jim."

Henry's next call was to Will. He answered on the second ring.

"Good morning Henry. You're up early. What can I do for you."

"I wanted to warn you that there is a poacher in our woods. I thought you should know so that you can warn your pride about going were."

"Thank you Henry. How do you know about the poacher?"

"He winged me. Doc Morgan patched me up and I promised him I would rest for a couple of days. Jim is in charge of The Fox while I am under the weather."

"What do you need me to do?"

"Nothing really. I just wanted you to know about the poacher."

"Does the sheriff know?"

"Yeah, I called them first. They must have called the doc because he was here when I came to. I guess I passed out while I was on the phone with them. I remember telling them I had been shot and then everything is blank until I woke up with the doc stitching my shoulder. I'm going to take one of the pills the doc left for me. The pain is getting pretty intense."

"OK you take it easy and I will have Chris or one of the girls bring you your meals so you don't have to lift a finger for the next couple of days."

"Thank you Will, I hadn't thought about meals. Thanks for thinking about them."

"That's why they pay me the big bucks." Will laughed and Henry chuckled along with him.

"See you later big guy."

"See you later." Henry replied.

CHAPTER 39

Will hung up the phone and went to find Chris before she left for her morning run. He found her putting on her running shoes. "Sweetheart, Don't go were on your run. There is a poacher in the woods. He shot Henry!"

"Oh my god! Is he going to be alright? How did you find out? Oh, wait, the phone call."

"Yes. It was Henry. He wanted to warn us about the poacher. Doc wants him to rest for a couple of days so I thought..."

"If he is resting then he isn't cooking so we should take him his meals."

Will chuckled, "I was just about to say that."

"Well great minds and all that."Chris laughed. "I'll take him his breakfast and do for him this morning. Then Jen can do lunch and I'll do dinner. How does that sound?"

"That my love, is perfect."

"Of course it is. I thought of it." Chris giggled at his expression. "I'll take my run later. I'll get the makings for his breakfast now and I'll use the Jeep to run them over. I figure I'll be gone a couple of hours." She leaned over and kissed him. "I love you. See you later." She headed for the kitchen.

Will sighed. He wondered, not for the first time, if Chris would ever stop surprising him. Then he shrugged. It really didn't matter. He walked down the hall to his office to call the sheriff's office and find out what was being done and what, if anything, he could do to help.

He was more concerned than he was letting on. Was the human really a poacher or one of the Van Helsing organization? They would have to find a way to question him.

CHAPTER 40

While Will was on the phone with the sheriff Chris was busy in the kitchen getting what she needed to make sourdough pancakes and bacon. She figured Henry would have coffee there so she need not worry about that. Picnic hamper loaded she jumped in the jeep and took off for Henry's.

Will called the sheriff's office and got a deputy who said she and the others were following Henry's backtrail to catch up with the poacher. He thought that they would be checking in when they were high enough to get a few bars on their phones or maybe one of them would radio in from one of the cars. The deputies searched walking in a line arm distance apart. Then they spread out and keeping each other in sight began to trace Henry's path from the house to the creek. There they looked for tracks that would indicate a human. Around a hundred yards from where Henry had fallen into the creek the sheriff found a discarded cigarette butt and could follow the odor of smoke and stale sweat that permeated the poacher's clothes. She whistled and the wolves congregated around her. They all got a good whiff of the poacher's body odor and began to follow the scent on two feet instead of four. They didn't want anyone else to be shot.

With the start the poacher had on them it was unlikely that they would catch him. Still it was possible that if he was intent on hunting and not running that they could find and arrest him. This was especially true if he didn't realize the bear he had shot at was really a human being. Will's mind was swirling with many questions about who he was and why he was in their area. The area was not noted for its hunting because of the ski resort. Snowmobiles and four wheel ATVs also frequented the area making game scarce. The engine sound frightened them. But it also warned the weres when they were out and about in animal form so they could avoid confrontations. Even the young learned.

The recklessness of youth was tempered by the need to belong to the pack and the pride. As a result the teens who were just learning to glory in their bi-nature were inclined to listen to their elders Not all of them were so minded but they were soon weeded out and the punishment for being seen as wolf was severe. The last wolf to allow himself to be seen had been beaten badly. That served as an example for the others who decided that discretion would overrule their tendency to rebel.

None of the teens had followed Jen's example and tried to journey to the east to see a love interest. There were too many possible mates in places like Yellowstone and the Black Hills or the Bitterroots or closer to home in the Sangre de Christos, places where packs went for vacations.

Besides the Elves were never around so far as they knew so there was no chance that any wolves would be smitten in quite the same way as Jen had been. It was interesting that the Elves were found to be nearly irresistible by all the other supernaturals. They were aware of the attraction and therefore kept to themselves. Especially since Jen's escapade! The only time they were seen since then was for council meetings and then they didn't socialize much. Humans who met elves were hopelessly drawn to them and they were looked on as pets by the elves.

The exceptions to the rules were the orcs and dwarves. None of the earth dwellers found the elves irresistible. Will wondered, not for the first time about the ignorance the humans were encouraged in following. The disinformation seemed to him to be short sighted. Be that as it may, he had a human to worry about and a pride to protect.

CHAPTER 41

The hunter could be a mercenary hired by the Van Helsings. He could also be what he seemed on the surface, a simple hunter after mule deer or whatever he could shoot. Still worrying at the question like an old cat with a bone was not very productive. It was time to send one of the wolves to investigate. The sheriff would know who best to send.

She called Will and let him know she would be visiting with the hunter that evening. It was her habit to swing by the restaurants during dinner to welcome new comers and visitors. Going to the Ramada would be entirely in character and she could be subtle in her questioning. She could also be quite blatant and direct. It all depended on quality of the person she was welcoming, read interviewing,

The sheriff was named Harriet Christian, Harry for short and she appeared to be harmless. She was five foot four and slender. Not much of a threat one might think, but she was also a black belt in taekwondo.

Her eyes were blue and her hair was chestnut brown. She was mildly attractive until she smiled and then she was disarmingly lovely. She went to the hotels in uniform and made much of welcoming visitors. She was actually interested in why people were in her town instead of Durango. The college was there and the narrow gauge railroad which was a big tourist draw. Her town had been busy during the gold rush as a staging point for prospectors. It was there that they got their mules and equipment and the supplies they would need for prolonged stays in the mountains hunting for gold and silver.

Harry wandered among the tables, gradually working her way to her quarry. He looked up when she stopped by his table.

"Hello, welcome to Silver City. I'm Sheriff Harriet Christian." She held out her hand.

He took her hand and she felt a frisson of desire. He had a surprisingly deep voice. He said, "Hello Sheriff. I am Johnathan Kincade."

"Nice to meet you. So what brings you to our town? Are you a prospector?"

He laughed, a deep guffaw, "Of a sort I suppose. What made you choose law enforcement?"

"Family tradition. My father was sheriff and his father and so on."

"Then your family has been here many years. Do you know any local legends?"

"How do you mean?" She asked, "We have the usual lost gold mine tales. That is why I asked if you were a prospector. We get a lot of folks during the summer who are here in the hopes of finding the lost mine like that couple over there." She pointed at a young couple across the room. They were dressed in obviously new hiking boots and western style clothes.

"Ah. I see."

She felt a mild popping sensation when she looked away from him. '*How odd,*' she thought, then she dismissed it.

"So you are here to gather local legends then?" She asked.

"Yes, in part. I teach a course in Myths and Legends at Yale. The Anthropology Department is my bailiwick and I would love to meet anyone who can fill me in on local stories."

"You should meet Henry then. He is our oldest citizen and knows all the local legends. I'll introduce him to you if you like."

"Why that would be great. I am particularly interested in Navajo and Hopi legends about skin walkers. I wonder does your Henry know any of them?"

"You will have to ask him. If you have finished dinner I can take you to the Fox and Hound where you can meet him and ask him yourself."

"Yes, I am quite done." He scribbled a signature on the guest check and threw a five dollar bill on the table. "I am ready to go if you are?"

CHAPTER 42

Harry was sure that he was more than he appeared on the surface and his question about the skin walkers was a dead giveaway. Also there was the frisson and the odd pop. She was looking forward to getting him alone where she could find an excuse to take him out of the picture. Maybe she could find a reason to arrest him. She could do that even if she had to invent a statute to support it. It wouldn't be the first time.

She wondered if he was here to discover the whereabouts of the missing Van Helsing members. She would find out as soon as possible. The Fox could close early to outsiders and then the weres could question him. She became aware that he was waiting for a response to a question. "I'm sorry, I was woolgathering. What did you just ask me?"

"I asked if going to see this Henry would be better in the daylight?"

"No, Henry is a night owl and sleeps during much of the day."

"Ah I see."

By this time Harry had isolated him and he hopefully had no idea that she was taking him to be interrogated. There would be nothing to help him if he proved to be a Van Helsing or their hire.

They arrived at the Fox and the atmosphere was much like that of an old English or Irish pub. The hunter, Johnathan Kincade, was impressed. He had expected a rustic honkytonk sort of place and not the immaculate sophistication he found. The place was nearly full to capacity and Henry was in his element. He had just finished telling a story about one of the early hunts and was receiving applause when Harry and Kincade entered.

Kincade was the only human present although he appeared not to notice. Harry wondered how much of what he told her was a lie. They would know soon enough.

"Well, young Harriet, what can I do for you?"Henry asked as she and the human approached. Henry caught a whiff of his odor and nearly snarled in recognition. This was the human who had shot him a few days before. His hackles rose and he fought the impulse to change and rend.

"Hallo, Henry. I brought you the hunter who shot you. I thought you might have some questions for him,"

While the human's attention had been on Henry the weres in the bar had been quietly changing to were form. Then one of the wolves moved to rub against Henry's legs and sit next to him on the floor. One of the cats did the same on his other side.

Harry then said I think he wants to ask you about skin walkers. The hunter finally realized his position and that his worst fear was being realized.

"What are you? Where did the dogs and all come from? What happened to the people? I didn't hear the door." He tried to sound ignorant and failed.

"Don't insult my intelligence." Henry demanded, "You know exactly where the people are." With that the weres next to Henry changed back to human form and making sure he saw them. "I believe you wanted to know about skin walkers?

Well it is time for you to learn first hand. Not that it will do you any good. You will either die or suffer the change yourself."The weres took turns biting him and what should have taken a couple of weeks of contact was accomplished in an hour, almost two. The bar was closed before that and the weres changed back to human after they bit Kincade. He laughed at them and said I have been hoping to have the opportunity to become other since I learned about you. I was hired by the Van Helsing organization to do precisely what you have just done. I was to become other so I could learn how to recognize you when you are in human form. There must be a way. Maybe your pheromones. There has to be something. How do you recognize each other?"

He suddenly looked surprised and then he doubled over in pain. He began to convulse as the conflicting were influences battled for supremacy in his system. He screamed in agony as the change caught at him and fluctuated between lion and wolf. He screamed and kept screaming as the weres looked on dispassionately.

"Well, I didn't expect the change to hit him so hard." Henry chuckled. "Harry I think he will either be a mixed were which is quite impossible or he will die. What do you think?"

"I think he will die. And I think it will take some time. The pain and convulsions will wear him out and he will die from it."

The convulsions stopped momentarily and a very humble looking human asked in a whisper. "What have you done? Kill me please."

"Oh I don't think so. But tell me what I want to know and I might."

"What do you want to know?"

"Who hired you and where?"

"At Yale and it was by letter. I never met the person who hired me."

"What was the return address on the letter?"

"There wasn't one." He moaned, "There was a phone number to call if I accepted." The check I got was a cashier's check with an unreadable signature. It was a hundred thousand dollars." He whined. As he bent over in pain the convulsions hit him again. He yelled from a throat already tortured by his screams. "Oh Gods! Please make it stop."

"Do think he is telling the truth?" Harry asked.

"I think he is too far gone to lie."

"Do you want me to kill him now or do you want to make him suffer some more?"

"I'll kill him. Zack or Jim? Hand me my pistol, please."

"No wait we need to have it be an animal attack so I don't have to investigate and the wolves are the ones to do it. I can report it as a wild dog attack since there is a pack in the hills. That will give me the excuse I need to hunt them down and

169

eliminate them. They have been attacking sheep. So everyone will be happy. Then I will notify his school about his passing provided he didn't lie about it."

"I see your point. OK. Jim please put the pistol back behind the bar." He complied with the request a bit reluctantly. He had wanted to kill the bastard. He supposed that a bear attack would be more in keeping with current happenings and said so. Henry perked up at that. "You're right, There are reports of bear attacks on campers once in a while and often enough that a human death at the hand or claws of one would be more acceptable than the wild dog excuse."

"Yeah, and you can always go after the dog pack for the ranchers."

"You can even call a general hunt for them and use humans to shoot them. We can join in the hunt in human form too."

"Yes, it will work. OK. I will call the ranchers and plan a hunt and I will make sure that we all know about it."

"There are most of the hunters here anyway so you don't have much notifying to do. Lets get this death over with." He said nodding at the whining lump on the floor. "We need to carry him into the mountains and then Jim and I can kill him when he goes human again."

"OK lets put him in the jeep in back and we will take him up to the next bear's territory, she is a female with cubs."

"Perfect." It was two AM when they loaded the convulsing thing, you couldn't call it human, into the jeep and they gassed up in town. The drive north was by back roads and so they avoided most of the normal traffic. Dawn came and they entered the bears territory. By eight o'clock they were near a berry patch of currants to attract the bear and her cubs so Henry and Jim unloaded the thing from the back of the jeep in time for him to go human again. He was drenched in sweat and his odor was overpowering.

Henry and Jim changed to bear and made short work of killing the hunter. They had stopped by the Ramada and gotten his back pack which they put on the ground next to his lifeless body. "Well that takes care of that." Henry said as they turned back to human. They scuffed out the boot prints and the tire tracks and left in the nick of time. Two berry hunters came on the scene and called the local game warden reporting the bear attack. Since there were tracks made by the female and the cubs nearby no questions were raised and no one went hunting a rogue. It was obvious that the mother was protecting her babies. The report was on the local news that evening along with recommendations for behavior when bears were involved.

Henry and Jim bumped fists and grinned at the report. "Yeah, avoid bear cubs at all costs or you may have to deal with a mutha of a mother." Jim said. Henry laughed and went to open the bar.

The bears were normally solitary so no one thought anything about the bear tracks near the body. It was assumed it was the momma bear. This was especially true with the disturbed scene. The berry pickers who had found the body had managed to muddy the tracks to the point that most of them were unrecognizable. The Game Warden who investigated the killing was sure that she had acted alone to protect her cubs. Fortunately she and the cubs had left the vicinity and he felt no cause to track her.

CHAPTER 43

Henry was tired. At his age a good night's sleep was a blessing he relished. Although in his case it was actually a good day's sleep. The exertions of the night and the lack of sleep made him cranky. So when he got a phone call at dusk he was just getting to bed. He snarled and thought about not answering but then he saw it was from Will. Since Will knew his sleep schedule he knew it must be important so he answered. "What is it?"

"I am sorry to wake you but we have a problem. There was a bear attack on a human and it was only six hundred miles away."

"No problem. It was Jim and me and it was the hunter who shot me. Ask Harry about it." He harrumphed. "Or ask your pride about it they can tell you, now I need to sleep I haven't had the opportunity until now. I mean, man, I just got home. And I drove all day. Jim drove us there and

I drove us home. Sorry if I am being rude but I am exhausted. I'll talk to you later. OK?"

"Yes, of course. Talk to you later."

Henry hung up without saying good bye. Then he set his phone to go to voicemail and staggered to his bed. He was asleep before he could pull up the blankets. It was dark when he woke up and he was chilled. He went to the bathroom and climbed back into bed. This time he stayed awake long enough to pull up the covers. He wondered idly why he hadn't gotten a call from Jim and then he remembered putting his phone on voicemail. He thought about checking his messages and the next thing he knew it was morning and he was hungry. A hungry bear is not to be messed with and Henry was all bear this morning. While his eggs cooked he checked to see if he had any messages. There was one from Chris and one from Jim from several hours before. He called Jim.

"Hello?"

"Hey Jim. Sorry I missed your call. Was it important?"

"I was just going to tell you about the night's receipts. We hit a jackpot. Apparently they closed the bar a bit late since we weren't there to call for last call. They finally closed the doors in time for people to drive home "in the dawn's early light". I think we can afford to take a day off or at least maybe I can? I'm pretty knackered. Gods yes.

I'll open and close for you. I'd best get on it. See you tomorrow."

"Thanks boss, I'll see you tomorrow." He hung up and Henry headed for a fast shower after he scarfed his eggs and toast. He was late opening and his wait staff and the cook and dishwasher were all there discussing whether they should call him or Jim to come open. There were already a few cars in the patron's parking lot. "Sorry I'm late." Henry said as he unlocked the employee entrance. He chuckled "I was more tired than I thought." The staff had been there the night before and laughed with him.

For the first time in a long time Jen and Richard came in and ordered steaks and drinks. Jen had her favorite Margarita on the rocks and Richard ordered a Sam Adams dark beer. They settled into their favorite booth where they could watch the coming and goings of the patrons in the bar. When any of the cats came in they would stop by the table and say hello, then they would move on to order drinks and food and find seats elsewhere in the bar. The wolves who came in were the deputies who had come off duty and were out of their uniforms. They were always given their first drink on the house, a practice Henry had instituted when he opened the place. He said that was why he had never been robbed. Everyone knew the sheriff's men and women frequented The Fox and Hound. Actually everyone respected

Henry too much to think of robbing the place but you would never convince Henry of that.

If it ever was robbed it would have to be by a stranger and the wolves and Jim would tear them apart once they were caught. And they would be caught! No one would ever find their bodies either. This was an unspoken covenant between them. There were plenty of deep mine shafts in which to place a dead body or rather the pieces of one. Many of them were known only to the weres. They were found on hunts and on rambles as the weres learned their territory.

Bears hibernate in the winter but the weres were an exception. They did sleep more but it was a natural healing sleep not the deep one of hibernation. They would sleep for the hours of darkness unless they had an employment requiring they be awake. Henry and Jim were of the latter weres. Instead of the hours of darkness they slept for ten or more hours during the day.

Without the necessary sleep they were extremely irritable and easy to rile. Their staff knew this and so were gentle in dealing with them. They also had prodigious appetites during the fall as their bear natures tried to develop the necessary fat to take them through the winter. By spring they were thin and felt like they were starving even though they ate during the winter. The calories needed to keep them alive during the winter burned away the fat they had accumulated during the late summer and fall. In human form they looked and acted like they were on a diet during the winter months. They found a strongly reduced appetite during the winter fit with their need to sleep more so in that they were very ursine.

Fortunately the early autumn that year was perfect for berries and Henry and Jim ate their fill. When Christmas rolled around Henry got his usual two quart jars of jam and two quart jars of jelly from the Deleons. He gave Chris a bottle of her favorite tequila and Will got a bottle of twenty-five year old brandy. Everyone was pleased with their gifts. Chris had to check out her tequila by making Margaritas. She pronounced it top notch and delicious. Will enjoyed a snifter of brandy and Henry had a hard time not eating a whole jar of jam. When he finally stopped dipping his hand into the jar and looked up his face was dabbed with jam. He caught sight of his face in a mirror and burst out laughing, so did everyone else. Chris was chuckling as she got him a wet towel for wiping the jam from his mustache and beard. They opened the bar for people who had no where else to go and he served a big dinner with ham and mashed potatoes and all the fixings. He served them wine too, all on the house.

Henry's generosity of spirit endeared him all the weres and humans who came into contact with him for any length of time. He invariably found some way to do them a favor. He found that doing favors ensured that he had help when he needed it although he seldom did. He had decided that it was time to turn the bar over to Jim and so this Christmas when everyone was gathered at the bar he gave the bar to Jim to general applause. He said, "I hope you will continue to hold holiday dinners here for those who have no family to cook for and that you continue to provide a safe place for our police to come for a drink after work. Aside from that you have free rein to run the bar however you wish. It is yours. I am getting too old to be keeping these late hours. I hope you will make me welcome when I stop by to tell a story or two."

"I don't know what to say. Except thank you Henry, thank you so much." He paused a moment. "Of course you will be welcome and as far as I am concerned this is still your bar. I hope you will be available to help me and to answer questions".

"I would be pleased to help out when you need it." Henry grinned widely and said, "You will probably get tired of having me hanging around, but I want you to know that I have every faith in you as a manager."

As everyone applauded Jim shook his longish cinnamon colored hair as he hugged Henry and said "You have been like a father to me and I want you to know that as far as I am concerned this is still your bar. I will continue it the way you taught me and that is a fact. You can take that to the bank." He paused, "Speaking of banks do we need to do anything about mortgages or titles or whatever paperwork there will be involved in transferring it over to me?"

"Already done. All you need to do is sign on the dotted line. There is no mortgage but they need your signature on the title and for signing the checks so you can pay your employees and suppliers." Henry laughed at him, "Oh, yes and you have power of attorney for me in case I can't take care of things for myself. I am more than eighty years old now and it is time for me to slow down a bit." He smiled, "Oh and by the way, Will and Chris will act on your behalf if you need them to." He nodded to himself, "Them or you can choose someone else you trust like Richard and Jen or even Harry."

"I think the sheriff is too busy with her normal duties to be bothered about me so I will use Richard and Jen. They are busy too but what's that saying? If you want something done ask a busy person? I don't mean to sound like I don't trust Harry. I do. I just think she would rather not get involved here because it could cause a conflict of interest."

"Um, I think you are right. I didn't think of that."He said ruefully, "I said I was getting old." He moved to sit in his favorite spot, a booth in the corner by the fireplace where he could watch the entire bar. "Still, I'm smart enough to know when I'm slowing down."

Jim looked fondly at the old man. "I think we will make that booth reserved seating so it will be yours whenever you want to come to the bar. I hope you come every night."

"Thank you, Jim. I think that is very kind and I appreciate it. I'll come often then. Now let's get this party going with some music. Anyone want to play darts with me?"

There were several volunteers and they did rock-paper-scissors to see who would get to play first. It was a young wolf named Jonas, who was middling fair at darts so he gave Henry a run for his money. Henry congratulated him on a game well played and then it was Chris's turn. Chris was not very good but then she hadn't played much. Henry on the other had had played every night for years. He won handily. He graciously told her that she showed promise and suggested she get a board and darts so she could practice. "If you have the opportunity to practice you will be able to beat me easily."

Chris was essentially a competitive person and the challenge was too good to pass up. She decided to go to the Walmart in Durango and to buy a set. Then she would practice before dinner every night. Maybe Will will play too she thought. *I really want to win.* That decided she turned her attention to the story Henry was telling.

It was the amusing tale of a first hunt. The young cat in the tale was clumsy in his first hunt and tripped over his own feet trying to run down a rabbit. "The rabbit would stop and look at the cat and then start running away when he got to his feet. After several fails the cat sat on his haunches nursing his bruised nose. He blew the dust from it and ignored the rabbit. The rabbit hopped closer to the cat. The cat still ignored the bunny until it was within springing distance. The cat sprang and tripped over his tail and rolled head over tea kettle. The rabbit ran helter-skelter for his hole and escaped. The cat nursed his sore nose and went home hungry. Fortunately his mother had made extra for dinner and he was able to fill his empty belly. He decided to listen to hunting lessons after his fiasco. His mother gave him a cold compress for his nose.

"Listening to instructions was important for the young." Everyone was laughing at the clumsy cat and they applauded the tale. Henry bowed, laughing along with his audience.

CHAPTER 44

The evening had worn to an end and the only people left in the Fox and Hound were Henry, Jim, Harry, Will, Chris, Richard and Jen. They were having a final drink when the phone rang. Shocking them all with a strident demand for attention. Jim reached behind the bar and answered. "Hello, Fox and Hound."..."Yes she is here, hold on a tick." He looked across at Harry. "Its for you." He said handing her the phone.

"What?"Harry began to tense, "When?"her hand began to shake..."Where?"..."I'll be there as fast as possible." She handed the phone back to Jim with a shaking hand. He r face was white and she looked stricken. "Its George. There's been an accident. He may not survive. They are airlifting him to a trauma center." She gulped and swayed in her seat. "He will never walk again even if he survives." She swallowed convulsively. "Oh God!"

"Oh my God!"Chris and Jen said together. "What can we do?"

Henry handed her a double shot of Bourbon.

"There's nothing you can do except pray for him. I'll have to go investigate but it sounds to me like his brakes were tampered with." She swallowed hard. "He went off the road at the hairpin on Wolf Creek Pass. It took a while to find him. They had to cut him out of the wreck." She drank from the glass and began to cough. "Holy crap! What did you give me?" She gasped as soon as she caught her breath. Color returned to her face.

"A stiff drink. You looked like you needed it."Henry stated mildly.

"Wow!" Harry exclaimed. "That was stiff alright. Thanks." She took a cautious sip. "This is sipping whiskey for sure. You got a chaser for me?"

"Sure." Henry said as he handed her a glass of water. "Here ya go."

"Thanks." She drank thirstily. "That's better." She chuckled ruefully. "Remind me not to fall apart around you again. You have a killer cure." Everyone chuckled at that and the solemn mood lightened slightly. "George would have laughed at me." She said sadly, "He would have called me a lightweight." A tear escaped to slide down her cheek.

"We need to decide who will go to the hospital and report back to us." Harry started to respond when he said, "It can't be you Harry. You have to conduct your investigation."

Chris looked at Will and he said, "It should be Chris and me. We don't have anything else going on and we are good friends/family, whatever."

"What about blood transfusions?"

"None of us can donate except for family members and he has the rarest blood type there is."

"George has donated several quarts for just this eventuality and we can transport it on the helicopter in a special cooler."

"I'll contact the hospital and let them know we have his blood type on hand and are bringing it with us. Let's get a move on." They split up then to take care of business. Harry to oversee the retrieval of George's car, Jim to close the bar and Will to arrange for immediate transport. Jen and Richard left to go home and to tell the rest of the cats about the accident while Chris packed for the trip to Denver.

Since they were carrying blood they were cleared to land on the hospital landing pad. There were nurses ready to take the blood and hurry it to be used for George. Will helped Chris from the chopper as the nurses rushed the blood to the elevator and down to the trauma center. No one questioned their presence so Will went to reception to give them George's insurance information and finish the check in process. The staff at the hospital asked no questions and Will was able to try to learn George's prognosis. It wasn't available.

Will held Chris while she cried quietly, "Oh Will! He looks so shrunken."She sobbed a bit, "He has tubes and wires everywhere. I saw him as they wheeled him into operating room. Oh, I'm getting you all wet." She sniffled. Will handed her tissues from the box on the table. They were the only ones in the waiting room so Will suggested than she stretch out on the couch and use his lap for a pillow. She yawned and said, "What about you?"

"I'll be fine my love, don't worry about me." He propped his feet on the coffee table. Chris laid down and was almost instantly asleep. Will turned on the television and watched an infomercial about the hospital. There were few channels to watch and there was HBO so he watched reruns of Game of Thrones. Apparently, they were running a marathon and they were only halfway through the first season.

Season three had begun before the surgeon came in to tell them George's prognosis. It wasn't good. "He should live but he will never walk again and that is the best I can tell you. We will know if he will survive in the next few hours. We have done what we could. At his age not being able to walk can be emotionally devastating. Especially for someone who is as active as he was. He is going to need all the support you can supply."

"W hen can we see him?"

"He is still in recovery but he will be in a room in an hour. You can see him then but whatever you do don't upset him. He will want to know about his condition and you are to tell him you don't know. I will tell him when his condition stabilizes. He is on a self administered pain management system. And he will be a little hazy from the anesthetic. Are there any questions?"

"I'm sure there will be but at this point I can't think of one. Thank you doctor."

Chris asked, "When will he be cleared to go home? We have much to do to get his house wheelchair ready."

"It will be several weeks. Perhaps as much as two months."

"Good. Two months? That will give us enough time to do a full renovation. I've been dying to give him a proper master suite."

"It will be nice to have decent size doorways that you don't have to go through sideways." Will joked. "I'll contact the architect today since it is Monday and he'll be in his office."

"Well you don't need to see me for that and I do have other patients. I'll check on him in an hour at the end of rounds."

Will and Chris went to his room, prepared to see him connected to multiple tubes and wires. They weren't wrong. George had a catheter and two IVs one for his pain and one giving him the last of his blood. There were wires attached to his head and chest and he looked oddly shrunken. It was because he was laying down Chris thought. He opened his eyes when they came in. "Hello Will, Chris. How are you doing?"

"We're fine but you don't look so good. Those shiners make you look like a raccoon."

"You should see the other guy." George joked. Chris laughed at that.

"You would make a joke about the devil if you were in hell." Will said. "Man you look like you were rode hard and put away wet. And that is being complementary."

"I know and I also know my spine is damaged and that I will probably never walk again so if I choose to make jokes I think that is just fine."

"How did you find out? George the surgeon wanted to wait to tell you."

"I heard the nurses talking about it when they thought I was still out from the anesthetic. I played possum until I could tell where I was. The last thing I remember was truing to brake on Wolf Creek pass and they failed."

"Man I want to see the car. I heard that they had to cut you free."Will said.

"Yeah I bet it doesn't look much like a car anymore. Is Harry investigating or do they think it was an accident."

"Harry is investigating." Will said. "She thinks they were tampered with."

"Yes and if someone did something to them she'll find them." Chris said.

"Yes she is a great investigator, a regular Sherlock Holmes." George chuckled. "I would hate to be on her wrong side. And whoever mucked about with my car will definitely be on her wrong side. I just had my car inspected and everything checked out in the green. She'll know that from the sticker on the windshield. That is if there is enough of one left."

"Do you have any ideas on who it could be? Maybe someone you put away who swore to get even? What about relatives of people with the death penalty?"

"Could be. I'll have to think on it. Usually the threats are bluster. No substance."

"Well this time it maybe had substance and I for one would hate to be in his or her shoes when Harry and the others catch up to them. Enough about that. How are you two doing? I haven't had a chance to chat with you for a while. How are the twins?"

"The girls are fine and planning weddings for the spring next year. We have met the young men and I do not see the attraction. But the girls are happy and that is what counts. Both of the boys are in excellent standing with the pride in California. The Cottonwoods Mountains are their home range over near Nevada."

"How are Jen and Richard coping with being mother and father of the bride twice so soon together?"

"Good question. I haven't talked to them about it but I know they are hoping one of them decides to elope and get married in Nevada. The cost of weddings has gotten ridiculous. You can buy a small house for what a wedding with all the trimmings costs.

"I guess I am lucky I dodged the bullet and never married. I can not even imagine raising children. Harry comes the closest to being my child as she is blood kin but she is not mine by birth just by love."

"I expect she will be in to see you as soon as she has a lead on your accident."

"Meanwhile I'll give some thought as to who has threatened me. I am wanting to go to sleep. It must be the pain medicine." George blinked slowly. I'll talk to you after I have a nap." And that quickly he was asleep. Chris leaned in and kissed his cheek. "Have happy dreams." She whispered.

"Shall we go grab some coffee and breakfast in the hospital dining room?"

Chris smiled, "Coffee would be wonderful and I could stand to eat too."

"We can ask to be paged when George is awake but I want to call and leave word for Harry and Henry and Jim about his condition first."

"Good plan and I want to talk to the architect this morning too and get him working on George's renovation plans. The sooner we get it done the better."

"Excellent."

CHAPTER 45

They found a bank of phones and began to make their calls. The first one was to Harry.

"Hello?"

"Good morning Harry."

"How is he? Uh...good morning. Sorry."

"He is going to live. He will never walk again but he will live. We are sending an architect to take measurements at the house for a total remodel and he should be there tomorrow or even later today. He'll need you to let him in, OK?"

"Yeah sure. I was going to come in to Denver today to see him but I can wait a day. We are still waiting for the car to be brought up so I can check it out."

"Harry, George said his brakes were just checked when he had his yearly inspection. They should not have failed so someone definitely messed with them."

"Does he have any idea who it could have been?"

"He said he would think about it after his nap. He was thinking a relative of someone he put on death row or someone with a long sentence who was recently released."

"I think there is a file with threatening letters in it. I will check that out too. Any thing that could lead me to the bastard who did this is worth checking out. George will have some idea of who it could be. I'll be in to Denver after I let the architect in to the house and he leaves to go make his drawings. Which hospital is it?"

"UC Health University of Colorado in Aurora. It is ranked number one so you know he is getting the best of care."

"OK I'll find it. Is he in ICU or where?"

"ICU."

"I'll see you later then. Where are you staying?"

"Comfort Suites, it's within walking distance of the hospital. Want us to book you a room?"

"Yeah, that would be good. Thanks."

"No problem. I still have some calls to make so I'll see you when you get to town."

"Sounds like a plan. Bye."

"Bye."

His other calls went much the same and he let the family know that they would be staying for a couple of days. He said to talk to Richard if there was a problem. And Jen agreed.

They stopped by a CVS Pharmacy to pick up toothpaste and tooth brushes because Chris forgot to pack any. They showered and changed clothes and went back to the hospital.

George was awake and seemed glad to see them. They told him that Harry was on her way to question him. He grinned a feral grin and said, "Smart girl. She makes a damn good sheriff." Will and Chris agreed.

They asked George if he had any thoughts on who might have damaged his brakes? Chris said, "I think it is the relative of someone you put on death row."

"It may very well be, although I don't remember anyone in particular."He sighed, "No one stands out and there haven't been that many. I only remember one but his elderly mother barely lived past his sentence. I don't remember if he had children. Harry may want to check that out."

"Harry is coming to see you. She'll be here later today. I think she wants to ask you about the accident and all."

"Where are you staying?"

"At the Comfort Suites. It's just a mile or so away so we can walk here from there. We got Harry room there too."

"You sure she's staying?"

"Yes. You wouldn't want her to have an accident because she fell asleep at the wheel."

"No, No I wouldn't."

"If Harry asks the wrong questions I feel comfortable giving her pointers. Or rather if she doesn't ask the right ones."

"I suppose so since it is you we are talking about."Will chuckled and George laughed too.

"You know me too well."

Chris laughed at that. "Yes, you could say that." She hugged him careful not to jostle the tubes and wires. "I love you George."

"I love you too Chris."

"So what do you want for breakfast?"

"Sausage, eggs and pancakes."

"Sounds good. I think I'll have the same, What about you Will?"

"Make it three,"

George rang for the nurse and asked her about breakfast. When he told her what he wanted she laughed and said, "You are definitely getting better. I'll talk to the doctor and see what we can do for you. You are healing faster than anyone I have ever seen." She shook her head. " Amazing." as she left the room.

"And that is one of the problems with being in a human hospital. Another one is blood tests. Changing to heal is also a problem. I am having issues fighting the change. I'm afraid I'll do it in my sleep."

"Well as soon as you are free of ICU we will transport you to home and the clinic there."

At that point the doctor came in and said "I need to check on my patient, if you would all please leave?"

"Yes, certainly." Chris and Will responded.

Harry said, "Yes and I will want to talk to you about my dad when you are done."

"Certainly, now if you would…?"

They left and went to the nurses station to wait. It wasn't long before the doctor came out and walked over to them.

"Your father is healing remarkably well and I can see him leaving the ICU in a few more days. I will keep monitoring him every few hours but he is definitely out of the woods. He even is hungry and wants eggs sausage and pancakes for breakfast." He laughed slightly. "Of course he will have to wait for such heavy food. I have OKed removal of the stomach tube and he can have cream of wheat for breakfast. I'll allow him coffee too." He smiled at Harry. "What did you want to know?"

"I wanted to know how long he will be in a wheelchair and is there any chance his spine is not as bad as you all think?"

"He has no feeling below his waist and when he tries to move his feet or legs there is no response. I would say he will be in a wheelchair for the rest of his life. I am sorry but I don't have any hope for a recovery. People just do not heal spinal injuries."

Harry swallowed hard. "I understand." An errant tear escaped her eye. "Does he know?"

"I would expect he does. He knows he has no feeling and he knows he can not move." He frowned, "I think he is putting on a brave face but you need to be aware that he will go through a serious bout of depression. I recommend psychiatric help when he goes home."

Chris who had been listening said, "I am a doctor of Psychiatry and I will be seeing him on a daily basis. I don't think there will be a problem with that."

"You relieve my mind. Although since you are a family member I would hesitate to recommend that you counsel him, still it is good to know that there is help readily available."

"Yes, I quite understand and I will give his file to one of my associates."

"Well and good then. I think if he continues to heal at his present rate he will be out of ICU in a week to ten days, maybe as few as five days. I will keep a close watch on his condition." He smiled at them all and said, "I have rounds to do and I will see you tonight or tomorrow when I do my regular rounds." With that he turned and went into the ICU room nest to George's.

The three went back into George's room. "You heard the doctor?" Chris asked. "I want you to know that it will be at least six months before you will walk again and it may be that you will need a cane for a while after that. At least although I recommend that you pretend to be in a wheelchair around non members."

"Yes, I agree.. The next six months are going to be hard and not being able to run with the pack will be difficult to deal with."

"That's where I come in." Chris said softly.

"I know and I'm grateful." George responded, "I am lucky to have a family and friends like you." George smiled and said, "Trust me when I say I will be smart about things. Now what about my car?" He coughed slightly "Were the brakes tampered with?"

"Yes, they were. We found where the lines had been punctured and cut and there was other damage too. You are fortunate that the car did not explode in flames which was the intent of the booby trap we found. The only reason it didn't work was that the person who placed it didn't really know what they were doing. It would take more than a Molotov cocktail to make it happen. They missed the vulnerable part of the car when they threw it."

"So you have something with finger prints?"

"No they must have been wearing gloves." Harry said frowning. "But we'll find them no matter how long it takes."

George smiled at her. "I know you will."

"Do you think they were human? You Have put humans away."

"I think it is likely. A were would be more direct. They would have gone wolf and attacked me."

"I suppose or cat or bear."

"Or coyote." This came from Chris. "We always forget about them. Do they even have a representative on the council?"

"Yeah they have one from Montana, not that he contributes anything to the meetings."

"Well at least they are represented."

"I am inclined to think that it is a human who jiggered my brakes."

I am inclined to agree with you." Said Will and Harry together.

George chuckled. "If I didn't have broken arm I would applaud. But enough speculation. I suggest we table any further discussion for when I am back home in Silver City. Agreed?"

"OK."

"Agreed."

"Harry?"

"What? Oh Yeah, OK."

"Did you know Lavender is expecting?"

"No, that's great news. Is it a boy or a girl?"

"I don't know. She hasn't found out yet."

"Well tell her congratulations for me."

"Of course but you can tell her yourself because they are coming home to have the baby."

"Are you as excited as you sound?"

"Yes, I rather think I am..."

"And so am I!"Will interjected.

"It is not every day one becomes a great grandmother. Jen is thrilled to be a grandma too. And I think it is very good of their California family to not mind about her desire to have her baby here. They may come out for the birth and they will stay with us 9if they do."

"Well I think it is grand!" Harry said.

"Thank you Harry."

It was at that point that the nurse came in and said it was time for George's bath. So she shooed everyone out. They told George they would come back during evening visiting hours except for Harry who would be going back home to spearhead the investigation. She kissed his cheek and said "We'll get them."

"I know you will." George said with a feral smile. He squeezed her hand with his unbroken arm and hand. It was the only part of him that wasn't damaged. She bent to hug him and elicited a groan, "Sorry sweetheart, My ribs are broken too."

"Oh god I am so sorry, George."

"No worries, my dear."

"I love you George. "

"I love you too, Now go catch the bastard who did this to me." He patted her hand and she turned away so he didn't see her tears.

Harry said good bye to everyone and asked Will to walk her to the elevator. "I want to have a police presence by George's room to vet everyone who wants to see him including staff. I'll set it up with the local force. I'll do it now before I leave to go home. Once they know he was our sheriff they will be more than happy to help." They reached the elevator and she pushed the call button. "Good bye Will. See the police know who to allow in, OK?"

"Of course, Harry. Bye. See you at home in a few days when we transport George home to the clinic there." The door opened and Harry got on, She smiled a bit wanly at Will as the door closed.

CHAPTER 46

Harry let her tears fall as she rode the elevator down to the ground floor. By the time the slow moving machine she had regained her usual aplomb and had wiped her tears away. She hurried to her car for the trip to the local police station and then the four hour drive home.

She was determined to have the attempted murderer behind bars or dead before George came home. As it was George looked to be in either the hospital or the clinic for at least eight weeks. There would be lengthy physical therapy for him to do so it was just enough time for the renovation of his home to be finished.

Harry arrived at the precinct and the first thing she did was check who among the humans

George had put away had been released and which ones had the knowledge to cut his brake lines. It was a surprisingly long list when she included the relatives of those still incarcerated. Time enough to start in the morning, She was drained emotionally and physically so she headed home and to bed. She was just too tired to make sense of anything tonight. Morning would be soon enough. She turned her phone to vibrate only and her alarm for six. She fell into bed and was asleep in nothing flat. Her dreams were unremarkable.

The first thing Harry was aware of was a pounding sound which seemed to be coming from her front door. She looked at the clock and saw it was a quarter to six. She groaned and turned off the alarm and went to the door. Curious as to who would be coming by at such an ungodly hour.

She looked through the window next to the door and saw two of her deputies. She sighed and opened the door. Her curiosity roused. "Good morning. Come on in. I'm going to make coffee. Do you want some?" She waited for her reply.

As she reached the coffee down from the shelf, she said, "So what brings you here so early? If I remember right you aren't scheduled to be on until eight."

"Yes, mam, we were called in to a situation at the Fox. Seems that some humans came in and were saying how a cop should know how to drive better than to go off a cliff. You see George's accident was on the news last night. Anyway they were set on by a couple of the local wolves in human form and they beat the crap out of the humans who went out and got a gun from their car. Things escalated from there and Jim had to pull out the shotgun. Fortunately it was loaded with rocksalt so when he shot them he didn't do any lasting damage. Anyway we were called in to quell any further trouble. We arrested the humans and called the EMTs to come see to them and the wolves who got caught in the crossfire."

Harry interrupted. "Anyone killed?"

"No mam. But young Andrew took one in the shoulder from the humans. He was there celebrating his twenty first and had more to drink than was prudent. The EMTs saw to him and our people first. Then they took care of the humans. Gave them bandages and called it good."

"Well, good job on your arrest. Now how many of our people were injured?"

"Five including Andrew. The humans are claiming that the gun discharge was a reaction to being shot by the rocksalt. Nonsense of course. Everyone swears they fired first."

"And you took formal statements to that effect?"

"Yes mam. But someone called the human press and they are wanting to interview the humans and the people who were at the bar. We have held them off so far but we thought you might want to make a formal statement about the incident."

"Yes you are right and I will want to talk to the humans before I do. I trust Jim knew what he was doing when he shot them. We are lucky that no one was killed. That would have opened a can of worms big time." She poured them each a cup of coffee. Now what is the word on the brakes and any finger prints?"

"We don't have a match yet but we have a few more to compare them to on the data base. They are being run as we speak."

"Good. Help your selves to cream and sugar." She finished pouring her cup and took a grateful swallow. "Do we have any leads other wise? Any of the humans or their relatives know much about cars?"

"We have a finalized list on them and there are more than I expected. You will be surprised at some of the names. Some of the more prominent human families are represented by teen age boys. And one girl."

"I was afraid we would have issues with the wilder set." Harry said with a frown. She was concerned about whose toes she would have to step on. The human population was small but they were wealthy and had political clout. She took another swallow of her coffee. Well they would have to be questioned eventually. It was possible that if one of them was involved they would be bragging about it with their cohort and be overheard by some of the wolf children. If that happened then the wolves would take direct revenge. Definitely not something she wanted to have to deal with. She prayed a silent prayer to any god who was listening.

"Please let it be a criminal or the relative of a criminal and not one of the human teens."

She couldn't tell if she had been heard or not. She hoped with all her heart that she had.

"Thanks for the coffee. We had best be going."

"I'll see you out. And thanks for the briefing. I'll use your heads up when I get in to the office. Should be in an hour. Its time to pull out the stops and blast full steam ahead." She paused then said, "Sorry about the mixed metaphor.."
She laughed and they joined in. "No worries Boss we know what you mean. See you later."

"Yep. Bye."

"Good bye." Harry closed the door and sighed. It was going to be a bitch of a day if she had to question the money set. Since they were minors they could have a parent present. Not something she was looking forward to. She poured another cup of coffee and put the empty cups in the sink to go into the dishwasher later.
She took the time for a shower and then used the blow dryer on her short fluffy curls. A touch of mascara and a quick dash of lipstick and she was ready to get dressed. She came out of the bathroom in time to hear her phone ring. "Shit." She caught it on the final ring. "Hello?"

"Good morning Sheriff. I thought I should call you. We got a match on the finger print. I thought you should know right away."

"Good job. Who is it?"

"You remember that wack job that Sheriff George sent to the state home for the criminally insane."

"Oh yeah! That one would be hard to forget."

"It is his print. Apparently he was smart enough to fool the shrink into saying he could rejoin society as long as he took his medications daily by coming to the hospital."

"You are not kidding me are you."

"No mam. He has been seen in Pagossa Springs. And one of our deputies said he saw him in town the day before the sheriff's accident. He didn't know to tell anyone at the station because the man was behaving normal."

"He was getting tools at the hardware store down town."

"I'll be in in a little bit and I'll want to ask him a couple of questions about his sighting."

"OK, I'll tell him to stay here and wait for you."

"Thanks. See you soon."

"Bye."

CHAPTER 47

Harry hung up and breathed a sigh of relief. Now to run down the nut case. She spent the time driving to the office remembering the case that involved the man. He had a genius level IQ she remembered and he was seriously bent. He started torturing small animals when he was a kid. It was his way of dealing with his fundamentalist, spare the rod spoil the child religious mother. As he grew up his focus changed to larger animals and finally human women. He was caught because he picked the wrong hooker for one of his victims. The other girls reported him to one of the beat cops. Because he killed one of their own. They described him as middle height, middle frame brown long shaggy hair and beard driving a Ford F150 pickup that had seen better days. One of them remembered part of his license plate, the part not covered in mud, and she told the cop. Since the crime took place in the county the town police called the sheriff and the rest was history. The sheriff and deputies finally ran him to earth when he was burning his latest victim, a teen aged coyote he had not given a chance to change. Not that he realized what he had.

George had done everything in his power to have the man sent to prison for life without the chance of parole. But he had a clever defense attorney and was sent to the state hospital called the Colorado Mental Health Institute at Pueblo Colorado. The CMHIP was an inpatient facility with nearly five hundred beds and dealt with mentally defective criminals from teens to adults. George would have gone to his hearings and given testimony keeping him incarcerated. Unfortunately he had not been notified of the last one and so the man was released. That set up everything that followed.

Harry called in a couple of favors from the state police and had an APB issued for the creeps truck. They ran the partial plate and discovered it had been reported stolen from a neighborhood taxi.

Harry put her deputies on high alert. She wanted him behind bars before George was brought home in seven weeks. He was her sole concern and so she was willing to ignore things like kids bombing mail boxes and paper boxes on the rural routes. And speeders who were only going a few miles over the speed limit. That is what she instructed her deputies to do also. If a speeder was going more than five miles over then, yeah, pull him over otherwise let him go. She told them, "I want you to keep your attention on ratty looking Ford pickups with possibly stolen plates. We know he has stolen them once so he may do it again." She sent her deputies out to hunt.

Now she had to play a waiting game. Days went by with out a whisper of a clue and then the pickup was spotted but by the time the patrol car got turned around he had been lost in traffic. Still it was a break knowing he was still in the area and then one of the human prostitutes came up missing.

He was back to his old tricks. Weeks went by before her body turned up wrapped in a plastic tarp. And by this time George would be coming home from the nursing facility where he had been getting physical therapy for his arm and hand. He was expected today and Harry could hardly wait. She thought about going straight out to George's house but decided that George would probably stop by the office on his way home.

She guessed right and around one o'clock Will's jeep pulled up out front with Will behind the wheel. She hurried out to help unload the wheelchair and get George settled in it.
He r next thing was to tell him that they had the information they needed to arrest the perp and who it was. He was impressed and asked why she hadn't told him while he was still in the hospital.

"I didn't tell you because you couldn't have helped with the investigation and you would have felt frustrated which means you would have gotten cranky with the people around you."

"What. Me Cranky?" He smiled to take the sting out of his next words. "I don't get cranky with any one, you must be mixing me up with yourself." Then he chuckled at her expression.

"Ooh, you!" She laughed. "I do get a touch irate don't I, when people are not doing their jobs."

"Yep." George smiled "But we wouldn't have you any other way. Now how about having some lunch with your old man."

"I would love to where do you want to go?"

"Where else? The Fox of course. I want some of Henry's Chili. I have been missing food with flavor. I swear that nursing home could make Jambalaya bland." He laughed. Shall we take my jeep? Or the patrol car?"

"Will do you want to eat with us?"

"Sure, that would be great! I'll just call the house to let them know we are back and that I am eating with you both at the Fox."

Call made they left for the Fox and Hound. George was welcomed with a bear hug from Jim and Henry came from the kitchen to share another. "We have missed you very much." Jim said. "I am glad you are back and will be coming in for your usual game on Friday night. At least I hope you will, it hasn't been the same without you."

Well tomorrow is Friday. I'll need someone to come get me until I can buy the handicapped van with the wheelchair lift and special controls. OK?"

"I have been playing so I can stop by your place on the way in if that's OK?"

"Sure I appreciate it. Now about lunch...You got any chili left?"

"Yep, I think I can scrape one up for you." What does everyone else want?"

"I'll have the same." Harry said and so did Will.

"Alrighty, three bowls of Chili coming right up. You want some coffee with that?"

"Coffee sounds great." I'll take a glass of milk too. The doc wants me to drink plenty of milk and take calcium supplements so we will need to swing by the grocery store and the pharmacy on the way home." He sighed then and said, "As much as I want to go home I am not looking forward to the stairs or those narrow doorways."He sighed again and said, "I don't suppose anyone made me a ramp out front?"

Will changed the subject before anyone could spill the fact that his house had been remodeled. He grinned and said, "I don't know. I didn't think of it. But I want to hear about your physical therapy."

"Yeah, what do they have you doing for your hand and arm?" Henry said as he placed the bowls of chili and crackers in front of each of them.

"I have a squeeze ball for my hand and I do curls and lifts with weights for my arm and rotations for the shoulder. To keep mobility I also do arm circles. Now let me enjoy my chili!" He commanded. Harry, and Will laughed and dug in to their own bowls. Henry went back to the kitchen to call to let everyone at George's place know to expect them in around an hour. Then he went about clearing up from lunch and prepping for dinner. Jim was busy washing the bar glasses and then he began stocking the bar for the night. "So, "he asked, "Are you gonna come in for the game tomorrow?"

George took a last bite of his chili, "Yeah, I think I will. I have missed our games."

"Good I'll stop by and pick you up," Will said. "Be ready around six and we can have dinner together before the game."

"OK I still need to go shopping for groceries and I am not looking forward to the condition of my fridge. There was a lot of food to spoil and go moldy while I was gone."

"Sounds like you could use a little help clearing it up. I volunteer to take the rotten stuff out to the trash bin." Will said. "I can hold my breath that long I think.

"Thanks Will, I was trying to figure out how to do it."

Will laughed, "Hey no problem. The cats and wolves will do for you until you are used to fending for yourself. Who knows with that claw thingie you have for reaching high cupboards you'll be self sufficient in no time."

"Good point I will be able to use my crock pot and microwave and the front burners on the stove and the oven." I think shopping will be a challenge since they don't take wheelchair bound people into account when stocking. I think what I may do is have them shop for me and then deliver."

"I didn't know they did that."

"Yeah, Hornbachers and King Soopers do. I understand Costco does delivery too." He grinned at Will. "I learned a lot of handy tricks to make my life easier from the therapy people."

"Well, I'm impressed." They pulled up in front of Georges house to an array of wolves and cats. Who transformed and yelled and applauded when Will helped George into his chair. Then they separated so he could see the gentle ramp leading to a wide front door. He choked up and actually cried he was so touched. Will said "Wait till you get inside."

CHAPTER 47

"What did you do?"

"Just go inside and look."

He rolled up the ramp and Harry opened his door for him. He stopped cold. "Is this my house? Are you sure you didn't bring me to a palace instead?"

"Harry laughed. "We were afraid we wouldn't get it finished in time. I think some of the paint is still wet." She laughed. "Do you like it?" I love it the colors are perfect and the open floor plan is perfect. Now what about the bathroom? Did you figure out a way to make it accessible too?"

"Sure go look we didn't move it exactly."

George looked at her quizzically. "What do you mean? Not exactly?"

The others involved in the renovation were crowding in to the front room of the house. They laughed or chuckled at his question.

"Go on! Go look!"

He rolled through his bedroom and didn't notice the adjustments there he was intent in making to the bath room before he had an accident. "Oh my!" It was all he could say. He slid the door closed and used the toilet. He washed his hands and realized the sink was lower and the faucet was elevated to make access easier. There was a paper cup dispenser next to a toothbrush holder it was all very elegant and looked like it belonged in a spa, the tub was one he could easily lever himself into and out of and had a rainfall shower head along with nozzles that would bathe him from every direction.

He was blown away and then he saw his bedroom. It was a master bedroom from a dream with beautiful stained glass windows behind the head of the bed and a fire place with a TV above it. There was a walk-in closet with all his clothes in easy reaching distance. He was truly amazed and he was so grateful he was speechless. He rolled out to the living area and when he saw the hopeful looks of everyone he knew they truly loved him. He cried unabashedly then and in a choked voice said, "I am so grateful to you all for caring enough to do this for me I...I..." He couldn't go on. Chris and Harry hugged him and kissed the top of his head. "Everyone outside donated to do it and the contractor did most of the labor for free. We really do love you, you know."The contractor was a bear from Boulder and came forward then.

"When your friends contacted me to do the work they told me what had happened and that they were raising the money to pay for the renovation. I have worked with the architect they were using before and I had a good idea what to expect from him. I think you will like the alterations in your kitchen too and we did make all your doors wide enough to easily accommodate your wheelchair. There is an elevator to get you to the second floor and the guest rooms with a Jack and Jill bathroom and your office. I'll take you up if you want to see it."

"Maybe later. I am truly overwhelmed for now."

The contractor grinned and said "I couldn't ask for a better response. The workers will appreciate it too. They put in unpaid overtime to be sure everything was ready for you today."

CHAPTER 48

"I am so grateful to everyone. Now we need to have a party for everyone involved." Lets see the kitchen. When he turned the women moved aside and disclosed a full buffet on the island.

There was beer supplied by the Fox and food from everyone including burgers and hotdogs done on the grill.

"Oh my. Let's eat!" He said and everyone lined up with the paper plates they had been hiding and took turns getting food. George was first and then Harry then the rest. People sat at the table and the floor, on the couches, chairs and they spilled outdoors to use the furniture and picnic table. Some found a seat on the ramp. Finally everyone had food and the hum of conversation made a sweet accompaniment to the meal. Harry turned on the stereo and found a great country music station. Those who had finished their food got up and danced and the party became more general as the beer flowed freely. When the sun set the outdoor lights came on and George began to yawn. He disappeared inside and thought about how to have the party wind down so he could go to bed.

CHAPTER 49

Will and the Contractor noticed the yawns and started telling people it was time to say good night and to go to the Fox and Hound or go home for the ones from Boulder. It was a long drive and they wouldn't get home before two or three in the morning. Reluctantly, they gradually found George and thanked him for the party and the chance to work on his house. They left a few at a time and within an hour the only people left were the local wolves and cats. The wolves came to George en-mass and said good night and then the cats finished cleaning up the residue from the party and said good night. The only people left were Will, Chris and Harry.

"Well Old Man what do you think of your house?" Harry asked.

"I am beyond words Harry. It is more than I ever dreamed of when I bought the place. I had plans to open up the dining room, living room and the kitchen but you fixed everything and the office is perfect and I love my bathroom and bedroom. I didn't know you had put in a bed that would raise and lower like a hospital bed until I went in to turn it down and saw the remotes for the Dish, the TV, and the bed. I am more grateful than I can say."

"As long as you are happy we are thanked." Will said. And Chris agreed. "Jim was only too happy to supply the beer to make the party merry." There were two or three apiece for the adults. There was also soda for those who were too young for alcohol. Although in the way of teens they managed to sneak some beer. There was not enough to get anyone drunk. And some of the adults preferred soda to alcohol.

"It was a wonderful homecoming. Thank you all so much. I know you are the ones responsible for this." George gestured toward the house and patio. You even landscaped the yard to make it easy care. I don't suppose any of the wolf pups would be willing to mow for me?"

213

"Actually that is also arranged with a yard care company...the same one that does the golf course. Unless you would rather have the wolves do it? I can arrange that too." Harry said. "Or you can."

"No I'll go with what is already arranged, but thanks for giving me the option."

"No problem dad. I expect we need to go now so you can get ready for bed. Do you want one of us to stay in case you need help?"

That would be good especially since I want to take a bath in my new tub. If you could stay Will? "

"Sure no problem."

"Good night old man," Harry said and she kissed him good night. "I'll call you in the morning."

"Good night George, I'm glad you are happy with what we did." Chris hugged him. "See you tomorrow. We are having lunch together. If you would like?"

"That would be nice."

"Good. See you then." She kissed Will and said "See you later love." She followed Harry to the door, then turned, and reminded Will to show George the security set up they had installed.

"Will do love."

George said, "Well lets do the security set up first then I can take my bath."

Will had gotten a state of the art security set up. Once it was engaged George's house

became a fortress. Harry had approved every bit of the installation and so had Will. There was no way anyone could approach within ten feet of the house without a quiet alarm sounding and the outside cameras turning on. Then George could either disarm the door alarm and turn off the proximity alarm or he could notify the police in the form of the sheriff's department about an intruder. This was automatic once the cameras identified a human intruder. They did not respond to animals smaller than a wolf or mountain lion.
George was impressed and said so. "This is great. I am safe even if I am asleep. I can relax now and wait for you all to catch the bastard who tried to kill me. Harry said that they had an ID and a description of his pickup".

"Yeah it is just a matter of time now. We are waiting for him to make another mistake and we will have him. Harry gave his picture to all the bars in the area with an alert attached so they will call as soon as they spot him. They will if they want to keep their licenses."

"Harry doesn't mess around does she?"

"No she sure doesn't. She loves you very much old man."

"Uh...yes, well she has to as my daughter." He paused a moment and had a misty eyed expression. Then he came to himself and said "Now how about my bath?"

"OK, lets do this."

CHAPTER 50

George wheeled into the bathroom and slowly managed to strip then he adjusted the water temperature and discovered that the tub was a Jacuzzi. He lowered himself into the swirling water and relaxed. This was a hedonist's dream and he was a hedonist. He washed himself after a nice soak and turned off the jets he was able to unplug the drain and climb out without help then he found the soft bathrobe that hung within easy reach and he saw that someone had put easy pull on pajamas on his bed. He thanked Will for staying and saw him out, then he set the security on and went to bed. He turned on the TV and Dish and settled back to watch the news. He elevated the head and foot portions of the bed and relaxed. He drifted off to sleep during the weather report. The alarm didn't go off all night. He was unaware that there were wolves patrolling his property perimeter. They had decided to do it until the murderer was caught and disposed of. There was no way he was going to escape their form of justice. The coyote even offered to help which surprised everyone. They were thanked and paired up with a coyote to a wolf. Of course there were very few coyote but the fact that they cared about George endeared them to the wolves. They learned that one of the psycho's victims had been a coyote and that was before George caught him. They were prepared to help kill the man and scatter his bones through out the mountains.

It was several days of waiting but it paid off when the sheriff's office received a call from the Spread Eagle, a DJ bar in Durango. He was there and sizing up the college girls for his next prey. The sheriffs sent their unmarked cars to locate his pickup and once he had it staked out the sat back to wait for him to come out of the bar. It wasn't long before he left alone. The cars were ready to leapfrog to keep him from realizing he was being tailed. They followed him to an abandoned storage facility and when he got out they got him. They took him to the sheriffs office and called Harry. "We got him." It was all they had to say. She said "I'll be right there."

CHAPTER 51

She threw on the first clothes she came upon in her closet and hit the door running. She hopped into the squad car and sped to the office. There were several vehicles and she realized that it was enough to hold a court. Because one of them was the local human judge. She arrived in time to hear the court being called to order. And she saw a badly beaten human being held upright by two of her deputies. She raised a brow and one of her men whispered that he had resisted arrest. The dash cam on the car would corroborate that.

The trial was swift. And the attorney who represented the killer did his best to make him seem a victim of child abuse which warped his thinking. He argued that he should go to the state hospital in Pueblo. But the District Attorney (DA) explained that he had been there and had managed to fool the psychiatrist into thinking he was cured as long as he took his medications and he promised to do that if he was released.

They had allowed him to leave and the result was more death. No one mentioned that George was alive until the DA said there was also the charge of attempted murder of the police officer responsible for his initial arrest. That brought the wolves to their feet and the judge had to call for order and bang his gavel several times. The defendant wove a fanciful tale of mistreatment in his childhood and misunderstanding by the women he had loved. Including the hooker he had killed a few weeks before. "They couldn't understand my needs." He said. The defense rested and the Judge charged the jury. They went to the back of the jail to deliberate and come up with a recommended sentence. They were back in fifteen minutes.

"The defendant please rise. Madam chairman have you reached a verdict?"The defendant was standing on his own and had a smug look on his face he was sure they bought his lies.

"We have. We find the defendant guilty on both counts and recommend the death sentence."

"So say you all?" The jurors all said they agreed when the Judge polled them. The defendant couldn't believe it. These country yokels had the temerity to call him guilty!

He reeled and started to run but he was caught handily by the audience and returned to here the Judge's words. "You have been found guilty by a jury of your peers and I find the judgment good. You are here by remanded to custody here until you can be transferred to the state penitentiary where you will be placed on death row to await death by lethal injection. If I could order you to suffer what you put your victims through I would. But we are a humane system and use the least painful means of execution available. I wish to thank the jury for their time and efforts and to excuse them. Court is adjourned.

CHAPTER 52

Harry felt gratified and told the Judge that she appreciated his time and efforts on George's behalf. "Well I can appreciate your need to have the trial in a speedy fashion. I understand George is home and will never walk again. I am truly sorry to hear that. He has always been so active. I will miss our golf games on Sunday afternoons."

"I didn't realize you were friends."

"Oh yes, for many years. The old wolf has always been a great friend. He is one of the few people I trust and that is because he has never tried to take advantage of our friendship."

"I understand. I imagine being in a position of power would be stressful especially with 'Friends'" She made air quote signs, "who feel their position allows them to request special treatment. I would hate that and I would probably tell them off and write them off."

"You have it in a nutshell." The Judge smiled at her. "That is why I respect George so much. It would never occur to him to take advantage of his position as my friend. To him I am just his friend from school. You know your father went to law school before he decided to be a cop. He passed the bar and worked a year for the District Attorney. That was when he decided to become a cop. He is quite remarkable."

"I think so too."

"Well I must be off, I have court in the morning. Take care and be aware that if Mr. Brown doesn't make it to the prison, I am sure he was killed trying to escape." He grinned a rather wolfish grin and shook her hand. "It was a pleasure meeting the daughter George talks about all the time. He really should have married your mother!"

"Not really, my mother was too high strung to be a cops wife. She worried about him enough as it was and they just dated."

"Well I must be off. Take care."

"Good bye Your Honor."

He waved a casual farewell and got into his jeep. It started and he waved again as he backed up and turned away to drive home to Durango.

CHAPTER 53

Harry went into the precinct and made sure her prisoner was lock up tight in his cell. Then she went to her office and collapsed in her chair. She tipped it back and put her feet up on her desk. Would her prisoner make it to the prison or would the wolves kill him and scatter his bones across the state? She rather hoped for the former and feared it would be the latter. If she had to, maybe to keep him alive, she should be his escort. But oh she was torn. As her father's daughter she wanted to deliver him to death row but as a wolf whose alpha was attacked in a cowardly fashion she wanted to tear him into tiny pieces. What to do? In the end she fell asleep as the sun was rising, decision made. She would escort him to prison. She woke a couple of hours later and ordered breakfast for the prisoner. She refused to use his name. Then she went back into the jail to check on him. He was lying on his side eyes open watching her.

"Are you hungry? I ordered you a breakfast."

He nodded. "I am so sorry about your boss. The sheriff was a notable adversary."

"Yes, he was a great sheriff." Harry realized that her prisoner didn't know that George was alive. She decided not to tell him. Lets see how far he will run with it.

"Yes, I would have preferred a person to person conflict rather than cutting his break lines and exploding his car. Still, I couldn't let him ruin my plans. Instead you did! I am not used to intelligent women. Most of your sex only think about shopping and their hair and nails. So I was surprised that you were the sheriff in his stead. That was my mistake. I did not credit you with brains. Still I wonder who they were talking about with the attempted murder charge. Maybe it was due to when I was hunting earlier last night."

"I couldn't find any non college girls and they were all having intellectual conversations. Not my prey at all. I should have stuck with the snow bunnies or tourists staying at Purgatory." Although they might have influence away from here and may have caused an uproar when they went missing I would have picked mistresses and hookers. They are generally stupid."

"Still I suppose in their way they are smart enough to capture the interest of the middle aged and wealthy. But they are not intellectually challenging and that sort of challenge I don't need. Intellectual women is a contradiction in terms."

"Really?"

"Oh yes, all women are good for is cooking, cleaning and making babies. They certainly don't belong in college. Still I suppose there is a place for them in society but I just for the life of me can't figure out what it could be, educating women is a waste of time and money."

"Well you may be right in some cases. But I have yet to meet the type of woman you prefer. In order to run a successful house a wife requires a strong ability to organize and to do math. She has to be a master chef and teacher. She must show compassion too and be an understanding companion who is ready to make love at the drop of her husband's pants."

"All in all she has to be a paragon?"

"Yes."

"Well you are a surprise."

She heard the door open and smelled breakfast. "Your food is here."

"Thank you."

"Um hum."

Harry returned to the main office and found a tray with her favorite breakfast. She took the tray to the cell and pushed it through the slit in the door for that purpose. She had removed the silverware and substituted a plastic fork and spoon, after breakfast she would take him to the prison and this meant going over Wolf Creek Pass. She planned on telling Brown that this was where George had gone over the edge to crash through the pines and hit the rocks below. The scar was still visible due to the broken guard rail. The drop was approximately fifty feet. Surely enough of a drop to kill a man.

223

She drank her coffee and ate the sandwich she got from the vending machine. It was egg salad. So it was suitable for breakfast. It was time to remove the prisoner and take him to prison. It was a quarter to eight o'clock and the office staff were starting to come in. She picked one of the men to accompany her and they took Brown out through the back door and straight to her squad car. Brown was buckled in in back and her companion got in front with her, She turned the car on and they were off to Canon City on East Highway Fifty. She put on the car radio and found a country station. Her seat mate began to sing along with the radio in a pleasant baritone. And she enjoyed the silence from the back seat. She checked on him in the mirror. He was busy looking out the window at his last views of the outside world. She thought he was storing up memories.

CHAPTER 59

Their route took them to Walsenburg then to Pueblo and then west to Canon City. It was a scenic drive and went out into the flat eastern portion of the state. The mountains rose on the left of the car and appeared to grow straight up from the dry grasslands. Once they reached Pueblo they picked up Highway Fifty that took them along the Arkansas River.

They had their paperwork signed by the judge and they pulled up to the gate. The guard came out and asked their business, then he saw the prisoner in the back of the car. "You have a prisoner to transfer?"

"Yep, all signed sealed and delivered."

I'll let you in. Pull up to the administration building and I will call ahead to let them know you are here. He was sweating in the heat and his odor was making Harry hungry. He smelled like sheep. Must be the uniform she thought either that or he was a type of were she didn't know existed.

She did as requested and two guards came out to escort them inside. While Brown was being processed she met with the warden and gave him the paper work. "We have plenty of room on death row for the likes of him. I'll see you out." He said "I heard about the car crash and the sheriff's injuries. I am sorry to hear it. I have heard good things about him. To bad."

"Well at least we caught the bastard who did it and we proved he killed the hooker from Durango and several others so he deserves what he is getting." The warden looked at Harry over his glasses which were halfway down his nose. "Yes he is. Well I'll take it from here. Will you want to come for the execution. The judge will probably come as will the DA and if possible I think other interested parties like his defense attorney. His mother is too old to make the trip. She had him in her late forties and he is in his forties now according to the paperwork." They had reached Harry's patrol car and the Warden said, "So long. I will send word when the execution will take place. His bruises and other damage will have to heal before we kill him so it will be several weeks. I figure he was resisting arrest?"

"Yes that is what my men said. Well we will see you in a few weeks then." Harry got in to the car and so did her deputy. She waved to the warden and pulled a U-Turn. She left the prison behind once she had cleared the gates.

She went west then to the end of the road where she took the road to Gunison and over to Ouray then through Silverton and Durango and home. The roads were curvy and the trip was beautiful. Her deputy sang most of the way home which made for a pleasant journey. She relaxed and the pain in her shoulders told her she had been more tense than she had realized.

She dropped the deputy at the station and drove to her dad's. She told him about the trip while he made spaghetti for dinner and she made the salad.

"I am proud of you for following through and getting him to prison. You were so angry that I wasn't sure he would make it."

"Neither was the judge, he said he expected that if he didn't make it alive it would be because he attempted to escape. Or at least that was the story he would expect."

226

In ten minutes the spaghetti was ready and they sat at the table to eat. There was beer or wine to go with it. Harry offered to do the dishes and George laughed. "No you run along home you look knackered"

"OK Old Man. Thanks for dinner. Good night." She kissed him and headed home. She would sleep better tonight than she had in weeks.

CHAPTER 60

A couple of months rolled by with nothing outstanding. George played poker with his friends in the back room of the Fox and Hound and had friends over for dinner and Pay Per View sporting events like Summer Slam as they enjoyed watching wrestling and Harry had a mild crush on Roman Reins.

George was in the Jacuzzi when he realized he could feel the water swirling against his toes. Within another two months he could feel his legs and had some measure of control. He proceeded to retrain himself to walk. But he kept it secret in case it was a fluke and he would be back in the wheelchair. He finally realized that he had done the impossible and had healed his spinal column. He decided that rather than it being severed it was merely pinched and the Jacuzzi had relaxed the pinch. He was in his living room when Harry came to visit and he showed her that he could walk. Not well but he could do it. She cried with happiness for him.

"Oh Dad I am so happy for you. When are you going to let others know?"

"I thought I would have a small dinner party and show off then."
You are invited and I think Will and Chris and Henry and Jim and maybe a couple of the wolves I play poker with. I haven't thought about others. I guess the people I invite will spread the word. And I will go on the Solstice Hunt. So everyone will be able to see my changed status. I will be a fully functional as Alpha again. I will invite the Coyote too since they helped hunt Brown."

"That is good of you, I should have known you would think of something to thank them. Maybe invite them to participate in the hunt? I expect they would feel honored."

"That's a really interesting idea, dad. You should do it. Even if they decline they will feel honored I think."

"I hope so. I don't want them to feel like I am being condescending."

"Oh surely not."

"I don't know Harry, they are touchy."

"Well you could bring it up during the dinner. Speaking of which do you want me to come early and help prep?"

"That would be great."

"OK when do you want to do it?"

"How about next Saturday night."

"Cool, I'll be here around three if that is soon enough."

"Oh yeah we will eat around eight but I'll want to do drinks and hors douvers around five or six."

"Sounds good. Now what about some lunch? I'm getting hungry."

"Sure I have some tuna salad made for sandwiches."

"Excellent, I love tuna salad."

Lunch went well as Harry filled George in on doings at the station and about the wealthy drunk she had pulled over who kept hitting on her. He seemed to be under the impression that she was a stripper and open to more personal service. She made it sound funny and George laughed.

"You meet some of the most interesting people as a sheriff." George said and Harry laughed.

"Yes you sure do."which led to reminiscences by both George and Harry. They spent a pleasant hour and then it was time for Harry to head back to the precinct, so she hugged her dad and left for work. There were a couple of drunks to release and a hooker to finish booking. She had come on to a sailor and then told him she was a grand a night. He complained to the bartender about the whore and they had to bust her for solicitation. She said she was just doing what she had read in a Pearl S. Buck story that was supposed to be true. She had said obviously it was a lie, and she didn't feel she should be arrested for a social experiment. Harry could see her point and was going to release her to go to her English class to tell her experience to the professor. She also thought the girl should write a paper for extra credit for her sociology class. She came close to siting the bar for allowing the girl to get so drunk but decided to let it go. She had just recently turned twenty one and did not understand her limit for alcohol.

Harry called her into her office and closed the door. "Now tell me again. What possessed you to try to apply a work of fiction to real life?"

"Oh but it was supposed to be based on a true story. It said so in our text. I just wanted to check it out but I shouldn't have used such a big amount. A hundred was what they had in the story. So that is what I should have used but then he could have afforded that and I didn't really want to do it with him. You see in the story the hooker asks if he is married and he said yes so she asked to see a picture. He showed the picture to me and I said what the hooker in the story said which made the man back off. It didn't work with him so I used a thousand dollars as my price. I don't know what I would have done if he had said OK."

"You were exceedingly foolish and all I can say is you should not drink so much. I am not going to book you so you will not have to appear in court, however I don't want to see you back here again."

230

The girl started to cry and said "thank you I promise not to drink so much again."

"OK. Now get out of here after you blow your nose and wipe your eyes."

"Thank you for giving me a chance."

Interlude

Harry watched the girl leave the office and wondered what the bartender would think if she had one of her female deputies go to the bar and suggest the bartender find her customers for which she would pay him a finder's fee. If he went for it she would wait him out and nail him for pandering when he followed through.

Well that was for the future for now she would enjoy her free time and going hunting with her father. She wondered what Will and Chris would do when they saw George walking. And she thought they would be as excited about it as she was.

CHAPTER 51

Will and Chris were pleased that George wanted them to come to dinner. Will picked a Rosé wine that would go with anything. He hoped that they would have something yummy for dinner like roast pork but he would settle for anything that was remotely edible. He knew George had a killer Spaghetti recipe and his Mexican food was

amazing. He had heard that George loved cooking so he was sure it would be good.
Will was more than ready to eat when they got to George's he knocked at the door and George called to come in. When he opened the door he stood stock still. George was standing by the stove.

Chris peeked around Wills arm and almost dropped the wine. "Oh George, You can walk!"

"I've been up for about a week now and I'm learning how to walk again."

Chris looked accusingly at Harry. "You knew all this time and you didn't say a thing."

"It wasn't my secret to share."

"Oh, I didn't think of that. Sorry."

"No problem. Dad is keeping this new development quiet for a while and only a very few will know until the next hunt."

"That's smart."

George laughed, "Glad you approve."Everyone laughed and the tension dissipated as quickly as it had started.

"We brought some wine that we hope will go with dinner." Chris handed the bottle to George.

"This will go nicely with dinner. I do like a good Roséé. Not as light as a white and not as heavy as a red."

"So what's for dinner, I'm starved, I missed lunch today."

"Here have some hors douvers. Dinner won't be till seven. We have some more people coming."

"Dad's poker buddies are coming."

"Oh I know them. I'm surprised they aren't here already."

A voice came from behind Will and Chris, "Who isn't here already?...Holy shit man you're standing!" It was one of the three men who were coming up the ramp.

"No! Is he really?"

"I'll be damned, shows you what the damn doctors don't know."

"Congratulations on a job well done, my friend."

"Henry's voice sounded from behind the men. "You want to move or are you taking up residence out here? Hi guys."

Every one made it indoors and Henry finally got to see George. He sat suddenly and said, "Well I'll be damned. When did this miracle occur?"

"I started having feeling about two weeks ago and then I started doing some exercises to strengthen my legs and now I can stand and walk a little." He suited action to his words and tottered to a chair. "As you can see I have a ways to go."

"But man you have a great start!"

"Thanks. I am doing a little more every day and by time for the solstice hunt I should be in good shape."

Chris said, "Well I couldn't be happier for you. You deserve to have all the help we can give you. I have some ankle weights that you can use to promote your strength building."

"That would be great. Now what does everyone want to drink?" And with that the party got going. George made Mexican food for dinner and made Sangria with the Rosé. The party was merry and the wine flowed. After dinner Harry loaded the dishwasher and they sat at the table and played poker. George won handily. Around midnight everyone was getting sleepy and since there were only two guest beds they said good night and drove for their respective homes.

Harry stayed over and made her dad breakfast in bed. Then she went home to change into her uniform. She was running late when she finally made it to her office to get caught up on what had happened during the night. There was nothing momentous. The usual baseball bats to mail boxes and paper boxes and the report of a group of boys tipping cows. Just another night in rural Colorado.

CHAPTER 52

Chris and Will talked on their way home about whether to share that George was able to walk again but decided that like Harry said, it was not their secret to share. "I am so happy for him

Will. It must have been a living hell being stuck in that wheelchair."

"I agree for someone as active as he was."

"So what do you want to do tomorrow?"

"Don't you mean later today?"

"Why, yes I suppose I do." She laughed. "I didn't realize how late it was."

"If you'll pardon the cliché time flies when you're having fun. And it was fun wasn't it."

"Yes I had a great time. I never did get the names of the others right but it doesn't matter."

"Nope."

They made it home around two AM and went to bed. Too tired for making love, Will curled around Chris and they went to sleep. They woke to Will's morning erection nudging Chris from behind and made passionate love, Chris said, "Thank you Will. It is always like the first time with you."

"That's because we love each other."

Chris laughed gaily, "Think so do you?"

"Yes, yes I do."

"Me too." And they kissed tenderly. Nuzzling each other in the way of cats, they fell back asleep. They had only had four hours of sleep.